# The Prescription Errors

# The Prescription Errors
## Charles Demers

SEROTONIN | WAYSIDE

**INSOMNIAC PRESS**

**Library and Archives Canada Cataloguing in Publication**

Demers, Charlie, 1980-
    The prescription errors / Charlie Demers.
ISBN 978-1-897178-86-7
    I. Title.
PS8607.E533P74 2009        C813'.6        C2009-904626-1

The publisher gratefully acknowledges the support of the Canada Council, the Ontario Arts Council and the Department of Canadian Heritage
through the Book Publishing Industry Development Program.

Printed and bound in Canada

Insomniac Press,
520 Princess Avenue
London, Ontario, Canada, N6B 2B8
www.insomniacpress.com

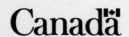

The Canada Council for the Arts since 1957 | Le Conseil des Arts du Canada depuis 1957

ONTARIO ARTS COUNCIL
CONSEIL DES ARTS DE L'ONTARIO

For my mom, Robin Demers.

*It is because of the body, not in the first place because of Enlightenment abstraction, that we can speak of morality as universal. The material body is what we share most significantly with the whole of the rest of our species, extended both in time and space.*

Terry Eagleton, *After Theory* (Basic Books, 2004)

*If the unexamined life is not worth living, he thinks, what of the life that is only examination, the life with no action that can touch a human soul?*

John Sayles, *Los Gusanos*

# I

The lights in the upscale grocery stores dotting this part of the city had a blue quality that put them closer to sunshine than fluorescence. In the brightness, a forest cathedral seemed to arc over the organic foods, fibrous cereals, and covers of check-out periodicals where news of the car crash had begun its slow bleed from the dailies to the weeklies. The vehicle was German, paid for in US dollars, but the talent was Canadian and so the story could lay claim to once-sober publications normally trading in cabinet ministers and transfer payments. Ty Bergen approached the magazine rack, glanced at the nearly pornographic images of a car, folded neatly in half around a street lamp, his eye drawn to a hole in the windshield, shaped roughly like an émigré comedy hero.

Al Sampson — an Edmonton boy who had skated poorly before giving up hockey; who had made his friends' Ukrainian mothers giggle because he preferred to eat perogies cold, from the fridge, as he perfectly mimicked their husbands' accents — had moved to Chicago in his early twenties to be an improv star, later pushing even further south to California. The old men at home, the ones who had never forgotten how bad he'd been at hockey, couldn't contain their pride or amazement: "And he just makes it up! He makes it all up right there on the spot, and they just love it!"

Ty Bergen pushed past the magazines, his grocery cart moving steadily forward, all four wheels ploughing straight ahead, in unison, and thereby belying a routine that he'd been doing for years: *These grocery carts, you seen these things? I can't be the only guy that's noticed this. The wheels on these things are going every which way but back in time, honestly. Where're they putting these things together, Sarajevo? Am I right? Where's this factory? I figure these things must be put together in Bosnia, since the wheels on mine are getting along about as good as the Serbs and the Muslims.* For years, Ty had considered the Grocery Cart Bit to be one of his best political jokes. It had been written when Sarajevo was a name that came to mind before Fallujah or Kabul. The shopping cart premise was a familiar one, worn by other comics before him, but he had found a new angle for himself and taken it.

Ty drew a sense of well-being from the grocery's lighting, though its effect was subliminal. He assumed that his sense of satisfaction came from recent financial news, perhaps heightened by the healthful, brightly coloured, and expensive foods surrounding him. Fairly Urban was a supermarket geared towards the young and upwardly mobile community that inhabited the condominiums spreading up from the marina and out towards Vancouver's downtown core, a territory that had itself been staked out by gay men, exchange students, and the homeless. The latter, Ty had been told, were known to lift the store's expensive cheeses. Urban legend held that, to meet the furtive requests of the owners of dingy pizzerias, the homeless would slip the blocks of imported cheese into the folds of their pungent vestments where no security guards would frisk. Ty smirked as he pushed his cart past the deli section, watching several young couples poring over cheeses, and he wondered which of them, if any, were secret shoppers. He stopped and took out his notepad. His pen left only blank indentations at first. He scratched violently at the crème-coloured paper, leaving a series of erratic lines on an otherwise blank sheet. Then he wrote:

Premise: Bums stealing cheese. Panhandling. Cheese grater. Mice. Three blind mice.

In the early eighties, Al had begun performing stand-up in Los Angeles, focusing — as Ty would, years later — on the wide range of impressions that were to land Sampson regular voice-acting work in children's cartoons. He met his wife Lynn, a writer, while working on a show called *Danny's Friends*, in which an anthropomorphized coterie of adolescent zoo animals attend classes with the zookeeper's son, Danny. Al and Lynn married in the summer of 1987, in Edmonton. It was her first time in Canada, and she met Al's childhood friends, then working construction on the third phase of what was, at the time, the world's largest mall. She had noticed how they would grip his shoulders tightly, innocently, with broad smiles.     She watched them loving him and trying not to be forgotten, hoping to get within sight of his new immortality. They wanted to know everything about Los Angeles, what the food was like and how often Al saw celebrities, what it was like to start a car without effort in mid-December. Their happy curiosity about the city would last only another year, until Gretzky made the same trip as Al had and the place became an enemy.

In the years when Sampson was voicing a zookeeper and a rhinoceros for Saturday morning audiences, an Oakland playwright and cartoonist named Phil Zavarise had put himself quixotically to the task of creating an adult-oriented animated series for prime time. *Army Brats* would be a wry satire, following the exploits of a Sergeant Brats and his military family, constantly uprooted and drifting from base to base like crewcut Bedouin, touring what Zavarise took to be America's pathologies. The titular patriarch would be imbecilic but sympathetic, paradoxically fey, trying manically, unsuccessfully, to keep his deracinated family together.

When Sampson landed the role of Brats, he had argued strenuously against his wife's suggestion that they move out of their ground-floor apartment and put a down payment on a house. *Army Brats* would be lucky to run for a full season, he had said; there was no adult audience for cartoons; in Reagan's America, no one was much interested in the Bay Area's drug-marbled and leftish political humour.

The program had earned and maintained a small following for two seasons on a young network, just barely achieving renewal with each year. But as the decade turned over, Zavarise's half-liberal nihilism found a place in the national conversation, when a compounded post-Watergate, post-Contra cynicism mixed alchemically with the international uncertainty wrought by the collapse of the Eastern Bloc. The dashed-hope fear that came with privatized markets and once-Soviet secessionists washed over an America without a foil to lean its goodness against, and *Army Brats* surged in the Nielsen ratings, becoming the anchor for its fledgling network. At the centre of the show were Sampson's myriad voices, voices no one could believe all came from one person, with infinite cadences and inflections and rhythms. They were voices rooted in a charismatic and almost-handsome performer who might even be dispatched to the big screen. The Canadian public had thrilled to the rise of a shining homegrown talent, making it big in the American markets, just as some now likely thrilled to the idea of such a profoundly American tragedy striking at one of their own. The success, the accident — all of it moved at speeds recorded in miles, not kilometres.

Ty stopped to weigh the relative nutritional merits of the bag of organic pretzels in one hand and, in the other, a sack of vegetable shoestring chips. He put them both into the cart next to his fresh-pressed apple juice and free-range eggs. His tiny yearly retainer was about to turn into regular, six-figure work. Maybe more, depending on what happened to Sampson. The time for choosing between groceries was past.

Ty had done his best to keep up with the accident: there had been a lot of trauma to his head, they'd reported, lacerations on his face, and spinal shock; Sampson was out and they had no way of knowing how long the coma would last or whether he would walk again. From what Ty had gleaned from a few hours trolling the Internet, searching Google and Wikipedia and various health sites, it would be impossible for Sampson to return to work without a fairly long convalescence, therapy, and even with all that, he might never make it back onto the show.

Ty moved towards the cash register, eyeing the items in

his cart, swerving at the last minute towards the frozen foods one last time. It had been so long since he'd bought ice cream. He picked up a four-litre container, not looking at the price, and made his way, again, towards the check-out.

"Sad, isn't it," said the cashier, a small, white girl with wide eyes, soft pink acne on her chin, and a crooked name tag on her apron. *Tanya.*

"What's that?" Ty asked.

Tanya nodded towards the magazine rack. "Al Sampson," she said. "He's Canadian, you know? It's really sad."

"Yeah," said Ty, producing his wallet. "I guess it is pretty sad."

Hours later, his groceries shelved at home and with night fallen outside the Brew Meadows restaurant and lounge, Ty surveyed the crowd at the tables: good-looking, affluent. West side people. He made his way towards the show's host, Shane Proudfoot, and nodded with his chin. Proudfoot had been the host of the comedy night at Brew Meadows for more than five years, through renovations, changes in ownership, and changed liquor laws. His stage had been in nearly every corner of the room, before settling on the wall opposite the bar. One particular set-up, which had placed the performers at the threshold of the women's washroom, had proven particularly deleterious for the relationship between the comics and their audience.

"Shane."

"Hey Tyler."

"Any spots open tonight?"

"I'm still waiting on Timmy Deacon, fucking cokehead flake. Fuck'im. You want his spot?"

"Sweet," answered Ty, raising his hand through a new haircut.

"Ty," Shane said, smiling with a degree of cruelty generally accepted among the fraternity of stand-ups, "are you wearing a ring?"

Ty curled his hand into a fist and smiled at his pinky.

"I am wearing a ring, Shane."

"Not just a ring — a *pinky* ring."

"That's right," he chuckled.

"You just find out you're part Italian or something?"

"No, no. Nothing like that. Not exactly."

Shane lost interest, turning back towards the bar to edit his set list, making room for Ty who always went past his allotted seven minutes, ignoring the flashlight shone from the back of the room as a warning.

"No, I'm not Italian or anything. The ring is just ... I'm coming into a few nice paycheques soon," called Ty. "Been letting my credit card out of the gate. Got some TV work."

"Nice. For who?"

"You know, the Sampson thing. The sound-alike gig."

"Jesus, that's right," said Shane, half-solemn. "Holy fuck."

"Yup," said Ty.

For four years, a deal worked out between Ty's LA representation and Bratspack Productions — the company responsible for *Army Brats* — had paid him a soundalike retainer, keeping his flawless impression of each of Sampson's voices as insurance in case *Army Brats* ever had to go ahead without its star. Now, mid-season, with Sampson in a coma, Ty's agent had been in touch with the studio to set up a recording schedule. Maybe even a move to LA.

"You're a jackal, guy."

"Yeah," said Ty, giggling nervously.

"Jesus, guy goes into the hospital…"

"Silver lining I guess, man."

"Yeah," said Shane, raising his eyebrows. "Silver lining. No shit."

"Yeah. They've got him in what's called a halo cast."

"Bodes well for you — makes it sound like he's already an angel."

"I don't — " Ty trailed off.

He leaned against one of the Meadows's load-bearing pillars, nodding at some of the other comics with his jaw, following the waitresses' asses with his eyes, scanning the room for shades of colour that might make a sampling of his accents forbidden for reasons of taste as well as the avoidance of altercations. *Fuck*, he mumbled, editing out his Corner Store Clerk when he spotted a massive, turbaned Sikh seated towards the rear of the crowd. The Sikh ran thick fingers through his chest-length beard and laughed along with his white tablemate at the comic onstage, Chris Mariner. The Sikh and his white friend were the only two laughing at Mariner's impossibly cerebral act. Ty had never seen Mariner do well in Kitsilano, though he'd killed a few times on Commercial Drive.

"A lot of people say that the seventies was the golden age of the movies," said Mariner into the microphone with an affected stutter, mic still fixed to the stand. "I don't, you know, think that that's true. There was no suspense in those movies. Like, *The Killing of a Chinese Bookie*. Right in the title, you know, they tell you how it ends."

*Fucking kid thinks he's Steven Wright*, thought Ty.

"Tough crowd. Or maybe, you know, just fans of the seventies? You guys — if you guys are fans of the seventies, you might like this new restaurant that just opened on the East side — you guys don't ever go to the East side, do you?" A few shouts of "No!" from the irritated audience. "But this place, it's neat; it's a seventies-themed diner. A seventies theme. You know, they got tired of all the fifties-themed diners, so, you know, they got this — it's a seventies-themed diner. Very authentic. It's an hour-long wait for anything cooked with oil.

"That was off the cuff, man, come on! That was straight off the top of my head, man. I used to do improv, you know. I was in an improv troupe that used the Kafka method. You'd be onstage acting, but no one would tell you the premise." Silence.

"You're up next," poked Shane over Ty's shoulder, already moving back to the bar.

"You don't have something later in the show?"

"You want a spot or not?"

"Fuck it," he said, though he'd always felt that seniority afforded veteran comics the dignity of a slot further along in the show. "Put me on, I'll clean up this fucking mess."

"I think this is going very well," said Mariner, and that got weak laughs. He took a long draw from a glass of water — *What the fuck comic drinks water?* thought Ty. *Take a beer up, fucking faggot* — and moved into his closing.

"You guys have been great. You love me. You love me like Paco loved Cupcakes in *Short Eyes*. But I am about to move into your collective subconscious. Speaking of which — have you guys heard that Naomi Klein is working on the definitive rebuttal of Carl Jung? She's calling it *No Logos*."

Nothing, just shaking shoulders from the Punjabi. "Come on, guys! Timothy Findley would have loved that joke — I mean *Carl Jung?* That motherfucker invented stand-up comedy! The differences between men and women? That was him! Men never want to ask for directions, am I right? Anyhow, this has been great; I always like to end big. Good night, everybody!"

Mariner left the small stage with a tepid sprinkling of applause from the diners, and Shane Proudfoot told two or three jokes to warm the crowd back up. As he did, Chris nodded hello to Ty, who sent the greeting back.

"Fucking university course lecture up there tonight," he said.

"What?"

"Big words."

"Yeah," smiled Chris, embarrassedly. "Thanks."

*Wasn't a fucking compliment, cunt.*

"You guys ready for your next comic?" Shane continued onstage, his gaze briefly following an attractive waitress across the front of the crowd. "This guy tours all over the place, he's done Just For Laughs, Aspen, he's done a Comedy Now special, what else? He's a scavenger. Just kidding. Please welcome, Mister Tyler Bergen, everybody."

Ty moved up onto the stage, smiling at Shane and whispering something nasty, sexual, and faux-spiteful in his ear. The crowd was hot. They were ready for him.

"Hey guys, hey everybody. Don't worry, you can put away your *Encyclopaedia Britannicas* now." Huge laughter, applause, and Ty grew in the spotlight, phototropic. Nearly six feet, he was handsome as the eyes took him in, though some women found that once they turned their heads, it was easy to forget what he looked like. "I keep telling Chris he ought to hand out maps to his references when he's up here. It's like reading the *Da Vinci Code*! Seriously — hey, I use the Da Vinci code for my PIN number; you think that's a mistake? I don't know. It's like," he says, shifting in to an ersatz-Middle Eastern accent, a vaudevillian arabesque, while the crowd hollers, rolls, and laughs, girls leaning forward to giggle and in so doing, exposing abstract tattoos painted on their spines. "'In the name of Allah, give us your debit code!' And I'm like, 'What the fuck do terrorists need seven bucks for?'" In the wake of this joke, Ty took a moment to savour the irony, letting the audience laugh as he paused to consider that soon any jokes about dwindling savings accounts would be pure performance. *I'm going to be Sergeant Brats, you fuckers.*

"You guys been hearing in the news about this lesbian children's book?" Collectively, the audience responded in the affirmative, some with applause, one of the fraternity boys in front shouting "Oh, no!" in anticipation and ducking his head into his girlfriend's chest, laughing. "This is, you know, there's this children's book, and it's by a lesbian, and they don't want it in the schools in Surrey, you know? And first of all, I'm like, 'They read books in Surrey?'" Big laughs at this. Any shots at the suburban bumpkins balms the Kits crowd's urbanity, flatters their sense of being rooted in a cosmopolitan echo of New York or Los Angeles.

"But yeah, this lesbian book, it's all about these two female turtles who fall in love. And I'm not making that up. And I know what you're thinking; we had lesbian children's books when we were kids, too, right, the little boy who saved Holland by sticking his finger in a dike. Honestly. It was

- 19 -

like, 'Huh!?!' But, so, yeah, this lesbian children's book, it's about these two dyke turtles. And my question is, you know, you're lesbian and you're a turtle — how much must you love the smell of fish?"

At first, the sound of the yelling was muted by the laughter and applause running electrically through the crowd, even the waitresses leaning back at their stations, covering their noses with fingers as though preventing a sneeze. And then simultaneously, in an action marked by the same unanimity with which they had laughed, the crowd turned its heads towards the back of the room, where a dissident had risen from his seat, yelling. It was the Sikh's white companion.

"Fucking shithead," he spat, and took his jacket from the back of his seat, his massive Punjabi friend rising as well, emptying bills from his wallet to pay the tab, taller than his friend even whilst hunched over reading their debt from the cheque. "Takes a lot of fucking courage, huh, shoulder to shoulder with the religious fucking — fucking *theocracy* out in Surrey, man. Way to pick your target, asshole," he said, growing nearly apoplectic, the Sikh now resting his meaty hand on his friend's shoulder. "You think this is what fucking Lenny Bruce would have done? Fight between a lesbian artist and religious fucking bigots and you're going to side with the bigots?" And with that, he shook off his friend's embrace, walking briskly towards the exit and pushing out. Ty stared at the Sikh, who stared back for a moment before leaving himself, but not before saying, "The last guy was funnier."

"Yikes," said Ty, deflating the awkward silence hanging above the room, and the remaining audience members melted into laughs of relief. "Um — you guys like impressions?"

The crowd cheered.

# II

In 1993 — a year during which I was thirteen and fat, and still assumed that the routine and repetitive prayers running through my head in constant ritual marked a devotion to God rather than a fairly severe case of obsessive-compulsive disorder — a journal called *Health Progress* ran an article titled, "Technology Decision Making: A Constructive Approach to Planning and Acquisition Will Require a Paradigm Shift." The two authors' names were Melanie Swan and David Berkowitz.

It struck me instantly as unfair: her name was white feathers and an emergence into beauty. A name like that, one assumes, guided you through life as in a cupped pair of warm hands. "Melanie Swan" was a name that would produce elementary-school crushes in boys and sign the cover letters that landed rewarding jobs. Conversely, her poor co-author was fated to share his name with the Son of Sam killer, the mailman David Berkowitz, the anti-Manson: a fat and unglamorous murderer, no friend to the Beach Boys, who took his orders from someone else's pet sounds.

Those were the sorts of details (the imagined biographies of authors, the injustice of names) that I noticed in the first phase of my pore through any literature that I could find on the subject of medical technology, before the spine had been broken on my medical dictionary.

The single margin notes entered alongside Swan and Berkowitz's article came beneath the heading, "Some Definitions." There, "Technology" had been defined as, "an existing, new, or emerging device, pharmaceutical, procedure, or protocol." Next to the formal definition I wrote in ballpoint pen "Old Testament God," a particularly appropriate notation, since it was the Catholic Health Association of the United States who published *Health Progress* (a journal whose titular makeup seemed, to a young man raised as I was on a secular Québecois father's Vatican-centred conspiracies, to consist of two decidedly anti-Papal words). Preparenthood Jehovah, I thought — an angry, jealous, vengeful God, as yet unsoftened by the birth of His Son and untainted by that theological analogue of minivan purchase, *forgiveness* — was an appropriate metaphor for the Technology that, over the course of my life thus far, had given and had taken away, and from which, all along, I had been alienated by a thick fog of mystification.

I was born three days early, with jaundice, plus feet turned either inwards or outwards. In any case, once I was released from the incubator I was in need of special baby shoes attached by a metal bar. Using the materials at hand to amuse his new son, my father would grasp the bar, hold me upside down, and swing me, making me laugh. I mention this only because — though I can't remember the incubator or the special shoes or whether my little feet were turned in or turned out — it seems significant to this story that my life started three days early with a disproportionate dependence on the whims of medical technology, marking a helpless and lifelong need for existing, new, or emerging device[s], pharmaceutical[s], procedure[s], [and] protocol[s].

From the start, and with precocious empathy, I nodded understandingly at kids with hearing aids or leg braces, knowing they were me by degrees, and figuring that once it was all finished my corpse would end up preserved like some sort of panicked jerky, frozen at an early stage of decay by the (un)healthy stockpile of pharmaceuticals pumped into my body from the moment the incubator's heat eased the yellow from my wrinkled skin:

- From infancy, constant ear infections keep my mother and me awake all hours and, from early childhood, my diligent gobbling of a daily prescription of antihistamines and Tylenol is the only way to avoid near-constant headaches caused by allergies and inflamed sinuses incapable of draining themselves. After three surgical attempts at fixing the problem simply create more scar tissue and more blockage, there come the constant nasal douches and saline solutions set to calm my sinuses (and it is then that I learn the concept of the "Vicious Cycle," driven home by a constant, subtly painful pressure pulsing out from underneath the freckles on my cheeks).

- At age nine, I am taken to the hospital for tests and learn that I am one of the province of British Columbia's few two-time cases of chicken pox. Incidentally, the scars from this — punctuating my almost-spherical Grade Eight body in the change room after gym — are taken by unkind Grade Ten boys to be acne. This pleasant fact of life makes me, likely, the only fat boy in the world who wishes that PE class would never end.

• The radiation set to kill my mother's cancer steals away her very red hair, replacing it with a kinky grey-brown that doesn't at all complement her nearly orange, freckled body, from which I inherited the surface of my painful and throbbing cheeks. In the time between the two follicular harvests, the treatment leaves her absolutely bald, a state that greatly intrigues and amuses my laughing little brother Marc, but which scares me so that I can't stand to look at her. In the subsequent years, the cure shaves her bones down to such a brittle lack of integrity that in the month just before I turn eleven she's killed by a sneeze that shoots her own ribs into her lungs.

*(I feel like I should apologize, here, for the unseemly sentimentality. This same pathetic sensitivity once had the adult me ejected from an irony-soaked hipster club — in actuality, a reclaimed dive bar, stolen from the jaws of the lumpenproletariat for kitsch value — for drunkenly shoving the lead singer of the "Emotherapy Cancer Ward Cleaver," a local band whose particular brand of middle-class cynicism bristled against my socialist realist earnestness.)*

• At the age of ten, I begin a regimen of twice-weekly allergy shots that mildly reduces my aversion to feather pillows while causing me to vomit volcanically every three or four days.

- As an obese adolescent of sixteen, I complain to my doctor about my constant exhaustion; he casually mentions that the allergy pills I am taking every morning on his orders are also prescribed to insomniacs to put them to sleep; I get off the medication and immediately lose fifty pounds.

- Just before throwing myself off the highway overpass at age twenty-three, I am diagnosed with obsessive-compulsive disorder and a major depressive episode; am prescribed 40 milligrams daily of the selective serotonin reuptake inhibitor called Paxil. No longer wanting to kill myself, I gain fifteen pounds in one month, and can no longer sleep or ejaculate. I withdraw from the treatment — a process that sends bizarre electric shock-like feelings through my body several times per minute for three days (an effect known, in online support groups, as "the zaps"). After gaining another twenty pounds over five unmedicated months marked by bouts of unstimulated weeping, I begin successfully taking forty milligrams daily of a different SSRI called citalopram.

In anticipating that switch to citalopram, I remembered with horrified immediacy the first nightmare days of the Paxil, the time for what the manufacturers have called "side effects," but which might better be described as kickbacks — my poor, lame-horse body bucking desperately against a new rider. On the third day of the prescription, for instance,

I had sat for twenty minutes, rocking fully clothed in an empty bathtub; over the next seventy-two hours I caught ghostly, green-white images of myself on reflective surfaces, and felt pangs of suicidal inclination, which had actually sharpened. By the weekend I was feeling better, but only after pushing through shakes, nausea, chilling sweats and stirring panic, regular vomiting, and evacuation of the bowels coupled with a trembling, gripping blueness that scared me shitless and therefore left me, as it were, both literally and figuratively without shit.

When the time came, then, to offer my bloodstream up to a whole new batch of pharmaceuticals, I begged my cousin Sara (who disapproved of antidepressants on healthy, hippie principle) to let me stay with her and her partner and their son for a week, there to be surrounded by the warmth of family as I adjusted to my new medication and negotiated what could potentially have been a new host of side effects. Sara warmly agreed, fixing a bed for me in her partner's writing room, leaving me late on the first night of my stay in the bluish light of the downstairs television while the rest of the house slept with the kind of heavy, pacific quality I'd always imagined existed behind the walls of other people's homes.

With the lights down, I sat on the couch wrapped in a blanket. Staccato channel-changing settled when I thought I saw warm shades of femininity, and what had until then been bored and aimless fingering took on purpose as I watched one of the hosts of late-night comedy interviewing some recently teenaged starlet. Turning my head to the left, I peered over my shoulder from the couch through the kitchen, out to the stained glass-enclosed foyer at the foot of the stairs leading up to the rooms in which my temporary housemates were sleeping.

My justification for what followed was that if the side effects of the Celexa were anything like those that I'd suffered while taking Paxil, tonight could be my last unlaboured, relaxed, and pleasant ejaculation for months. Still fresh were memories of abusing myself to rawness, lying atop a cooling pool of my own sweat, not even enjoying an exercise that had ceased to be about pleasure and now had everything to do with simply releasing pressure. So I couldn't help but take advantage, here, of television's late-night depths. Wadding an excessive ball of Kleenex into my left fist, ringing my pinky around my testes, I pumped the rest of myself in a grip now tightening, now loosening. I relieved myself embarrassingly quickly and took several more sheets of Kleenex to dry any excess. My obsessive-compulsive fears — in this case, the imagined toxicity of my semen, and the fact that Sara's son played and watched TV and experienced, generally, his boyish innocence within these walls — trumped any environmental concerns, and so, I loaded my hands with the easily-disposable, gently-scented white tissues to prevent disaster.

Mother Nature dispatched instant karma with an avenging swiftness. Once I'd dropped the wasteful, guilty mass into the toilet, flushing exhibits A and B of my tacky auto-eroticism, the toilet rejected the evidence as inadmissible, too bulky to be swallowed and thus to be returned.

"Fuck," I exhaled.

Crouching to close the flow, I tried to shut the valve but turned it the wrong way, wetting the floor with a rank cascade of pregnant water and deflowered Kleenex. Right-ing my latest wrong and shutting off the water properly, I looked for a plunger (none) and checked for ragged enough towels for the job of soaking up Shame Lake (none again). Cursing louder than I meant to, I ran upstairs to Sara's room, tapped on the door and opened it without waiting for a response, the smell of sleep punching past the broken seal.

"Sara," I said.

"Daniel?"

"Sara, sorry. Where's your plunger? And, like, some rags?"

"The plunger is in the ensuite," she answered sleepily. "And there's a bag of new rags under the sink."

"The sink downstairs?"

"No, sweetie, in the ensuite, too."

"Thanks," I said, making my way stealthily across the room into the bathroom she shared with her partner. The plunger next to the toilet was strangely dainty, a white head tapering to a clear handle filled with beach pebbles. As close to a nice-looking plunger as one can come, I supposed, before moving into marble or something. Even then, the marble could only make up the handle — even the very rich would need rubber heads on their plungers. In the small cupboard beneath the sink, I found the bag of "new rags" that I had been instructed to employ: a sack of her son's old white tube socks, cut into strips. I ran back downstairs to the seminal mess I'd left marooned in the bathroom, the toilet now surrounded by polluted water like a first-year art student's critical take on his family's summer vacation to Venice.

I sunk the white head of the plunger into the water,

robbing it of its beauty, pumping the rubber against the porcelain hole with a rhythm sickly reminiscent of the dance that had put me here in the first place. The water soaked my bare feet as finally the Venetian throne swallowed and gurgled successfully, draining the bowl and letting me turn my efforts to the floor. I opened the bag of sock elements that I'd taken from the ensuite, letting a handful of them fall onto the floor's wetness and, for a moment, I watched them mockingly float like origami flowers in a stream.

"Fuck," I said, just loud enough, it turned out, to roust Sara from bed in her nightie. Looking over my shoulder aghast, she immediately ran for the mop and some old towels. Before I knew it, she had put herself to the task of sopping up my mess, a ridiculous scene exacerbated in its ludicrousness only by the irony of my initial intention in using so much Kleenex: To keep anyone from coming into contact with what I imagined, in an obsessive-compulsive haze, to be my deadly sperm.

And I would say that as much as any anecdote can do, that pretty much catches you up on who, essentially, I am. That, and knowing that even though my namesake walked into a den full of lions, *I'm* allergic to cats.

Swan and Berkowitz explain that "a technology assessment program is not complex, but it does require time, information," and in my case, as an impetus, such a program requires a tear-soaked, anxious collapse at a Hallowe'en party occasioned by the sight of an acquaintance dressed in a surgical mask. At such a moment, senses flooded with vivid memories of standing bedside, age seven, with a thin, yellow-paper mask pulled over my tiny nose and mouth, hooked behind the ears with white elastic, knowing it was the only thing keeping my mortal, seven year old's germs from killing my mother.

I met Dave, who co-hosted the Hallowe'en party with his young wife, Lydia, while we were both working as summer students on the spare-board at the Scott Paper mill in New Westminster. Lest anyone mistake the town — with its hookers and drug dealers and strip clubs (like the poetically named "Mugs and Jugs") — for the area surrounding the Abbey, with its Isaac Newton tomb and what have you, I'll repeat that this was the *New* Westminster. Dave and I had spent the summer months tensing our shoulders as boxes came down the rolling, half-automated conveyor belt in the dank shipping building, reading Trivial Pursuit questions without the board and ducking our senior co-workers' racism and outrageous misogyny during down times. We'd spent one ten-hour shift together cleaning machinery saturated with a molasses-like substance, using high-powered air hoses and an endless supply of paper towels. In a moment of industrial whimsy, I had turned the hose against the inside of my forearm, admiring the fluid, vibrating crater that it produced, until Dave explained that I might blow an air bubble into my veins that would kill me upon reaching my heart. Years later, it was explained to me that this was not the case. At the time, however, I was inclined to believe Dave, because his summer wages were paying for a technical education during the scholastic months of the year.

Dave's wife Lydia — who kept, next to her alphabetized bookshelf, an immaculately handwritten list of the books she eagerly lent out to friends and acquaintances — was a graduate student in history, studying Ukrainian immigrants and migration patterns in the Canadian Prairies. The thesis that she had been working on for three years compared the fate of immigrant Communism in two Western provinces, BC and Alberta, and when she'd found out that I had old family friends named "Gidora," she begged me to set up an interview, citing a passion for oral history. The weight of my sloth, and the resulting reluctance with which I moved to set up the meeting, stifled the passion.

The Hallowe'en party itself, held in the ground-level suite of the Vancouver Special that Dave and Lydia shared with their upstairs Portuguese landlords, was like most parties thrown by MA students: a baker's dozen sampling of their academic cohort, with five or six outsiders awkwardly negotiating jargon-laden conversations centred nervously around approaching deadlines and poor organizational skills admitted to in fits of manic laughter. As her fellow students teased Marxist Lydia, celebrating their own worship of Foucault or even Butler, I made my way over to a snack table that, like the cacophonous conversation surrounding it, was emblematic of young academe: When the somehow indigenous-looking, thick earthenware dishes had run out, simple plastic plates and bowls had been brought out to offer up a host of snacks running the full spectrum of a sophistication determined by ethnic authenticity (*samosay* and *pakoray* on the one end, Triscuits at the other). At the table, I began what started as a fairly successful flirtation with Tracy, a short, thin Chinese girl dressed as a pirate and opting for Triscuits. She explained that she worked as a researcher at the Centre for Clinical Epidemiology at the general hospital, knew Lydia from salsa classes years back, and then proceeded — earlier than most would — to voice aloud the suspicion that every savvy Asian woman in Vancouver harbours in relation to white men. She smiled as she said it, though, and the heat of the wine and flirtation had softened the accusation like the microwaved, fruity brie that she spread, smiling, onto her cracker. My response was mock sleazy:

"I understand what it is that you're getting at, gorgeous, but I want to assure you — and I understand the politics of it all, I promise, and I'm totally down," and she laughed, and as she did she ran her tongue up across her top lip, shaking her head like, *No, no you aren't.* "But you don't have to worry. I don't have a fetish. I'm not that type. I've never applied to teach ESL. I don't even know what *manga* is exactly."

"Is that right?" she asked, with her tongue now literally in cheek, and it filled me up halfway that she played along.

"Sure, absolutely. Look, you don't have a thing in the world to worry about. No, I date all kinds of girls. Chinese, Korean, Thai, Japanese..."

"So, right," she says, laughing. "You don't have a fetish at all. You're like the United Nations."

"Let me tell you something, sweetheart," I say, putting my drink down on the table in front of her. "In a city full of white men with the whole Asian thing, I am proud to say that I exoticize no one."

"You must be very proud."

"Most of the guys I know, fuck it, every guy in Vancouver, they all have stories about the night they drove out to see the strip clubs in Richmond — "

"Right," she said. "I've heard this."

"That's right. Because they think — "

"They think the strippers must be Asian in Richmond."

"Right," I repeated. "They think the Richmond strippers must be Asian."

"And?" She says, widening her eyes and smiling.

I shook my head solemnly, and she laughed. She had a sweet, nose-wrinkling laugh, which was too bad, as I had run out of funny things to say. Another run at the fetish joke would sound desperate, creepy; if I had too much material on the topic, too great a familiarity with it, it might confirm her initial reticence. I scrounged desperately for another joke the way you search pockets for bus fare during an unexpected downpour. Feeling the conversation cool, I took another tack.

"So, have you worked long at VGH?"

"Oh, we're talking seriously now?"

"Sure," I said, motioning her towards the loveseat, far enough away from the grad students for conversation.

"I've been on contract there since last April."

"So that's not bad. Is it interesting work at least?"

"It's good, yeah, and it's in the field that I studied, so, you know — "

"That's all you can ask for."

"It's true," she said, and then repeated herself wistfully. "It's true."

I felt myself slipping into a *keen* persona — the Super Interested in What You Have to Say mode into which men slide when they've set too kinetic a standard for wit in the early minutes of a flirtation and need to back away from the pace that they've set for themselves. The conversation began to veer into the banal, useless small talk, and thoughts of VGH brought my mother to mind as Tracy started scanning the room for more interesting interaction.

"So how do you know Lydia?"

"I told you already, we took salsa classes."

"Right. Sorry, yeah, you did." The pirate's eye patch she had worn at the beginning of the night now hung loosely around her neck, and she held it lightly and absent-mindedly as her interest waned.

"Could you hold on a second?" she finally asked, and as I nodded she disappeared into the kitchen, and I stood to take a long toke from a pipe held by a spaceman seated cross-legged at the coffee table in the middle of the room.

With failed flirtation and macabre thoughts of childhood sitting on my chest just as clearly, to my mind, as the "S" on the five-foot lesbian dressed up like Superman on the couch underneath the Gustav Klimt poster — which I was surprised to see; don't they repossess those from the girls who still have them once they get their bachelor's degree? — I excused myself to Dave and Lydia's room, to lie down in the dark on everybody's coats and to work myself into a fit of stoned anxiety.

While some get paranoid, the OCD-case has full, grimacing, silent conversations with mirrors when he's high; the terrifying loss of one's (already-illusory) control over one's thoughts is too much to handle.

The obsessive-compulsive has a pathological inability to push past the mental dross and debris that his healthier counterparts are able to ignore in a sort of Nietzschean sublimation of the violent impulses and perversions coursing incessantly through the mind. An obsessive-compulsive, such as myself, can't move beyond the dark lapses, the left-field thoughts — "What if, instead of helping this old lady put up her missing kitty poster, I pushed the thumbtack into her eye?" — that the rest of you have and then ignore, maybe even laugh off, rightly, as absurd. We're arrested by them, obsessed: paralyzed by background images like some poor sob sister who can't get off the couch after seeing a World Vision commercial.

And that, mind you, is with all faculties intact. Once you're high, forget it. Perspective erases itself totally, and memories of trauma become just as fresh as the present is clouded, coming into greater focus just as the hard edges come off of reality — so much so that when you open the door and see Dave's brother, Peter, dressed as a surgeon with the paper mask drawn loosely over his mouth and nose to cover the laughter with which he's trying to fill the hallway, your heart seizes and your eyes fill with tears too quickly to notice Tracy kissing Lydia's cheeks goodnight.

Excusing myself to the bathroom, I rushed desperately to restore some semblance of balance and to coax myself out from the arms of hysteria with palmfuls of water to the face and, in so doing, ruined the thick, painted moustache whose subtraction made my conceptual costume (for Lydia, I'd come as "Russian Democracy") nothing more than a McDonald's uniform underneath a rabbit fur hat. With a machine-gun panic I racked my mind for resources with which to combat the onset of psychic collapse, finding nothing in religion, life lessons, or parental wisdom. My heart rate picked up into what felt like a goose step, amplified by the grass into thunderclaps up the sides of my neck. Sucking in tears, with shaking shoulders, I saw the fragrances and rosy powders on the countertop and remembered the unreturned book that Lydia had lent me most recently, part of her Left missionary work: *Cosmetics, Fashions, and the Exploitation of Women*, a mostly unsubtle hammer and sickle job on the makeup industry, fed through the lens of a very particular reading of Marx's theory of commodity fetishism. My breathing slowed.

I remembered how when I'd first come across the theory, it had taken some time to size it up. There was its relation to the alienation of labour, part and parcel of the assembly line Marxism that disappeared when all the blue collars were sent to wring necks overseas and serious people in North America stopped talking about political economy. Seemingly more relevant to life après-NAFTA — an "information economy" of ideas, and especially *feelings*, plus flipping real estate — was commodity fetishism's exploration of the ways in which we let material goods stand in for social experience.

In order, therefore, to find an analogy we must take flight into the misty realm of religion. There the products of the human brain appear as autonomous figures endowed with a life of their own, which enter into relations both with each other and with the human race. So it is in the world of commodities with the products of men's hands.

Like a twentieth century grandson of peasants, I set the man Che Guevara apparently called "St. Karl" onto a problem religion couldn't fix for me, breaking down my traumatic experience into line-items. I steadied myself against the bathroom counter. How could the benign wishes on a purchase request form filled out by an orderly hold this kind of power over me almost twenty years after the ink had run out of the ballpoint pen he'd used? Gradually, by reverse-engineering this obscure trick of *Kapital* — by thinking of the scarring experience as nothing more than a collection of amalgamated objects whose totemic power was authored only by me, completely arbitrarily — a calm and detachment set in.

1. IV
2. IV stand
3. Linens
4. Bedpan
5. Wheelchair
6. Hospital gown
7. Paper masks

When I was about eleven years old, my friend Stephen was prescribed glasses. After they'd arrived, he wore them over to my house triumphantly, and I couldn't have been more jealous. To me, the glasses made him look older, smarter, more interesting, and so I asked him what I could do to damage my eyes to the degree that I would be able to join him in his bespectacled sophistication. He advised that I watch television pressed up closely against the warmth of the screen.

With Stephen on the couch behind me, new glasses tucked behind ears which were, as of then, still outsized against his small face, I kneeled in front of the television — not "kneeling before the TV" like some Grade Ten English-class metaphor, but actually sitting on my heels in front of the old Baycrest with the thirteen channels and the false wood panelling that sounded hollowly when knocked upon

— and let the images honeycomb across my field of vision, too magnified to be taken in. That was the first time I ever looked harder, closer, and more intensely at something in order to achieve blindness. I was just a kid, then. I'm an expert now.

In his essay "The Personal and the Collective Unconscious," Carl Jung reported on a patient who had immersed herself in knowledge to escape feeling. Now, a lot of people think of Jung as having been weak-kneed in the face of Nazism, a fact which is germane to this case only in that it offers you a glimpse of just how ecumenical I'm willing to be, cherry-picking the tools of neuroses from both ends of Modernism's totalitarian divide:

> ...the patient's peculiar relationship to her father stood in her way. She had been on very good terms with her father, who had since died. It was a relationship chiefly of feeling. In such cases it is usually the intellectual function that is developed, and this later becomes a bridge to the world. Accordingly our patient became a student of philosophy. Her energetic pursuit of knowledge was motivated by her need to extricate herself from the emotional entanglement with her father.

Now, in fairness, the bridge that *I* was interested in building led *away* from the world, but that seems to me a matter of idiosyncrasy. Personal preference; superstructure, not infrastructure. Whatever the case, I think I deserve a little credit for crossbreeding Marx and psychoanalysis into something so toxic as to make Marcuse and Zizek look like pussies.

Some days after the Hallowe'en party, I started looking

around on the Internet: IV stands, hospital gowns, search-ing for how it was that they came — physically — to orna-ment trauma in the first place. Nowadays, the responsible parties would simply go to an aggregating website and order equipment through the organizational miracle known as "e-procurement."

I started thinking what it must have been like when Mom was in the hospital, the same year as Expo. Nurses fill-ing out forms in triplicate, carbon copies, ordering different equipment from myriad sources, plus pens, pencils, Wite-Out, staples. It was a whole other way of doing things, and they did it with no sense of the revolution on the horizon, wholly absorbed in soon-to-be obsolete work, like poor-sap monks two-thirds into transcribing a Bible at just the same moment as Gutenberg is copping his brainwave from the Asians.

Mom had died in a past historical bloc, and the proof was in the distance that technological advance and the re-organization of labour had put between us. How could I keep mourning across such a vast expanse?

O

I didn't normally charge Sara for babysitting her son, Robe-son, a little white boy raised by lesbians and named for one of the great Renaissance men of the twentieth century, Paul Robeson, the actor! the athlete! the operatic singer! And most importantly, the Communist! The great timbre of that man's voice shook the world and was an enormous contrast to the shy and trembling eight year old who sat on my couch, scared frozen by the film we'd just watched, one whose title I was trying to convince him not to share with his mothers when they picked him up. Seeing as Sara and Nicole were *paying* me to look after the boy tonight (a good-will donation inspired by the special brand of pity reserved for poor relations), I figured it would be pretty shitty if they found out that I had traumatized sweet Robeson with an age-inappropriate movie selection. The irony was — with his head pushed back against the couch, eyes dropped and blank like that — he looked more like the kid from *The Shining* than any of the characters from the Kubrick that we *had* watched.

"Remember, Robeson, it's just a movie," I called out from the bathroom in my tiny East Vancouver basement suite. Hunched over the sink, I took my head pills with a sip of water from the tap. There's no diminutive for "Robeson," which is tough, because I needed one.

Sara and Nicole arrived at half-past ten, and I kissed each on both cheeks (Nicole's puffed and reddened from crying) as Robeson sat, still shaking, on the couch.

"Hello," sighed Sara, her long auburn hair pulled back into a ponytail that reached nearly to her tailbone, and seemed even longer when next to Nicole's high bun, pulled tight to highlight wooden earrings. My cousin and I share a taste for the Rubenesque: Sara's small, pointed breasts and straight hips stood in remarkable and appealing contrast to Nicole's breathtakingly full-hipped, heavy-breasted, and slope-shouldered form in a crumpled, papery purple dress.

"Hi," I said. "How did the meeting go?"

"We'll see," said Nicole. "Not so well."

Sara was more visibly angry than her partner, her face

animated with fury as she made her way into the kitchen, rummaging in the cupboards for a clean glass while the tap ran to cold. She settled on a mug.

"It was fucking bullshit, Daniel. The meeting starts, and like always, there's one parent there who's the ringleader, yeah? And he's just the most sickening, perfect caricature of these ignorant, suburban alpha — He's just going on and on about "gay recruitment," and he's just absolutely over the edge ... And then the meeting proceeds and we find out that he's the local pastor, and that more than half the kids, the white ones anyways, are his on Sundays anyhow! And so it's like, we can fight until we're blue in the face to make sure that the book stays in the library, but he's got every weekend to make sure it never takes root."

"Jesus," I said, helpless. "Did they ban the book?"

"They decide later," explained Nicole. "Tonight wasn't meant for that. It won't be for months, maybe next year even."

Nicole had written and illustrated a children's book called *Turtledoves*, a story about Shelley and Slowey, two girl turtles ("*gurtles*") who spend their time asking questions of their fellow pond animals about their homes, and end by sharing a shell between the two of them. While the book had faced no serious opposition here in the city, some of the Parents' Councils in the more religious, rural areas and suburbs were opposed to allowing stories dealing with "same-sex issues" — Turtles! *Sharing a shell!* (Keep in mind I haven't left anything out about anal beads, okay?) — into the elementary schools.

Nicole and Sara had been out tonight at a parents' meeting in Surrey, where, apparently, one of the local pastors — whose children attended the public elementary school after the private religious facility that he had administered had run into tax problems — was trying to make political hay by leading a high-profile campaign against the book's presence. For months now, these kinds of fights had been taking the wind out of Nicole's sails in particular, siphoning hours of sleep into waking anxiety. Having been crying, likely since leaving Surrey, she now reached into her purse for eye drops, a mnemonic visual cue that elicited an excited whimper from Robeson on the couch, and signaled to me that my shortcomings as a babysitter might soon be readily apparent.

"What's wrong, Jelly Bean?" asked Sara.

"Oh, it's nothing," I answered for him. "He's just a little scared from the movie we watched tonight."

"Aw, don't be scared, Jelly Bean," said Sara as she smiled and bent to kiss the boy on his forehead. "Do you want a little glass of milk?"

Robeson again emitted a muted shriek, this one more panicked than the last. Sensing that something was very wrong, Sara turned to me and asked, suspiciously: "What movie did you show him?"

"It was nothing, I — " I was stammering, ashamed. Darting my eyes from side to side evasively, I was distracted by my reflection in the hideous, gold-veined mirror near to the entrance of the kitchen and I was thrown, foggy-headed, into reluctant honesty. "A *Clockwork Orange*."

"What?" Sara screamed. Her eyes peeled open in an anger that shook her long ponytail as she shot herself erect.

"You showed him *A Clockwork Orange*, Daniel?" asked Nicole.

"What in Christ's name is the matter with you?"

"I had forgotten — I'm sorry. I was in and out of the room, I don't know. He liked the cover, and he really wanted to see it, and I'd forgot — I forgot just how — fuck — I didn't remember how bad it was."

"Daniel!" screamed Sara, driving the stake further into my heart, "*Singin' in the Rain* is one of Robeson's favourite movies! He loves that song! What is wrong with you? He's eight years old! Don't you remember how shook up you were at his age by *Lord of the Flies?*"

In fact, I had been ten. Back then, around the time that my mother died, my friend Vito's father had shown us a contemporary film adaptation of Golding's opus at a sleep-over. Vito was my best childhood friend, my next-door neighbour (surely "best friend" and "next-door neighbour" are synonyms until age eleven at least?) and we were each half-and-half kids who identified only with our stronger-flavoured ethnic roots. Regardless of the equal parts Irish and Scottish running through our veins, we were Italian and Québecois, respectively, wearing our Romantic fathers' surnames (not to mention Vito's *al dente* Christian name) as proof-positive.

Our houses had been built by the same people, in the sixties, and so the layouts were identical: Visiting Vito was, therefore, like experiencing an Italian translation of my own home — the same dimensions, only filled with couches and vases that had seemed hyper-modern for a month and a half, and were after that nothing more than gaudy throw-backs, evidence of someone's semi-fascist Mediterranean vision of a future that, thank God, had never happened. They had a kitchen with the window in the same place, but the room smelled of onions instead of nothing. Vito would retrieve porno movies from the deeply engraved, ornate, and monstrous cabinet in his father's room (whose counterpart, at our place, housed my Anglo grandmother's Hummel figurines), and play them while I shuddered at the sight of enormous, throbbing, veiny cocks that looked nothing like the tiny pink protrusion in my pants, the one dwarfed even by my own modestly sized, hairless balls. *Pussy Pumpers*, though, was only the second most traumatizing film that I was ever subjected to in the midst of the Little Italy next door.

Vito and I had gotten into a fight downstairs in his family's basement one afternoon over a play-car that we had imagined, made out of his heavy red couch, with a drum skin from his father's set for the steering wheel and a drumstick for the gearshift. In order to explain to us the necessity of orderliness and democracy in decision-making, his father rented *Lord of the Flies* and made us watch it.

I had been terrified by the picture, mostly because I was at that time the hated, youngest, fattest member of a frustrated suburban baseball team whose roster fit Golding's cast of characters with an eerily accurate parallel. I remember it washing over me the way my Grade Eleven English teacher defined an Oceanic Experience — a sudden burst of meta-consciousness wherein I, the dugout, and the chalk lines leading from base to base became one, and understanding set in with a cloud of terror calmer (yet deeper-set) than the breathy panic of normal pre-teen fear. Kenny, our coach's son, was an easy Ralph, and the sociopathic Brody, our tallest, best-looking, and most violent player, was Jack. *I was Piggy*. And I remember, all of ten years old, realizing that if the Burnaby Metro Mosquito Division baseball squad, in our white, green, and yellow uniforms, were ever stranded on some tiny tropical island, I would be dead within days, a shattered conch and bloated corpse the only evidence that I had ever even existed.

My fear of Brody's truly violent and malicious potential was confirmed, two or three years later, when he and a group of other boys stomped our neighbour across the street with such brutal abandon that the black-and-white newspaper pictures of Peter, their victim, could only be described as cartoonish when they appeared the next week. A few nights before the beating, Peter had come across a group of teenagers (like *neighbour* for *best friend*, "teenager" was shorthand for "violent thug" on my block, and not wholly without reason) vandalizing a construction site just down from our place. A few days later, when picking up his kids after class, he recognized one of the young men, smoking a cigarette outside the school.

Middle-aged men castrated by Saturday morning soccer do stupid things. They are aware that, having accomplished little by way of athletics or art or politics in their time on earth, their final chance at glory or notoriety is to be the freakish, accidental hero of one of the emergencies of quotidian life. Peter chose to pounce on his destiny (read: this kid with the cigarette), thereby inviting the boy's friends — standing in the wings and led by Brody — to stomp him within an inch of his life with the shoes that their parents had bought them.

His face collapsed in on itself. Giant purple-brown circles obscured his tiny, red eyes. Stitches railroaded his cheeks and forehead. His jaw remained wired shut for weeks. Some time later, Brody's horde threw a bottle through his living room window, just to let him know that they knew where he lived.

I sighed in relief that our team had never played any road games, but was unable to so much as look at the cover of Golding's book all through high school. Retrospectively, it had become clear that at least part of the terror had been the result of my as-yet undiagnosed mental illness. The OCD that I would only later be given pills and counselling for, at this early time, had the island boys' savagery running on a constant loop in my mind's eye for months, maybe more than a year, and so I had long since considered the *Lord of the Flies* trauma to be a product of something altogether more particular than simple childhood sensitivity.

And yet here, now, was poor Robeson, wetting his mother's shoulder with mucous and tears, and talking about "that man shaking in the wheelchair." It wasn't too late for somebody to drop a rock on my head.

"Look, Sara, Nicole, I'm really sorry. I don't know what was — I'm sorry, okay? I — I am so sorry."

"It's not us you should be apologizing to, Daniel."

"I know. Robeson? Buddy?"

Robeson turned his little tear-soaked mess of a face up to look at me, which reminded me of how much, in fact, I really did love him, even while envying his maternal surplus in a world of orphans and quasi-orphans like me.

"Robeson, buddy, I'm sorry, okay? But you don't have to worry about any of that, okay? It's just pretend, all right? It's just a movie. I don't want you to worry because nothing like that is ever going to happen, okay? I love you buddy."

"Come on, Jelly Bean. Let's get you home to bed."

Nicole scooped Robeson up into her arms, while Sara kissed his head on their way to the door.

"I'll be right out to the car, okay, honey? I just need to talk to my cousin for a second."

"Okay," said Nicole. "Good night, Daniel. Say 'Good Night' to Uncle Daniel, Robeson."

"Good night, Uncle."

"Night, buddy."

After I had shut the door behind Nicole and Robeson, I could see the sensor light through the kitchen window as they turned up the small pathway that led from the back of the house to the front. The sympathetic, condescending look on Sara's face indicated that this postscript was to be on a different subject than that of her recently scarred son.

"Daniel, are you still taking those pills?

"Oh Jesus fucking Christ, Sara ..." Sara, a good leftist, hated that I took anti-depressants and could not be dissuaded, even by the now-exploded psychological fragility of her own son, from taking every opportunity to express the fact that, from her healthy vantage point, she couldn't fathom my prescription. "I am not going to have this debate with you every single time that I see you. I fucking can't!"

"I just want to know if you got that piece on Paxil that I forwarded —"

"I'm not even *taking* Paxil anymore. Jesus, Sara, where is this indignation about capitalists in the pharmaceutical industry when I ask for an antihistamine because of hay fever?"

"Daniel, there is no —"

"No, fuck it. I'm completely serious, Sara. This is — I feel you are, you know, jeopardizing our relationship with this shit, okay? I can't think of any more, whatever kind of, you know — way of telling you this. I can not take this from you constantly." Sara's eyes began filling like her son's.

After my mother died, Sara's mom, my Aunt Patricia, had played the primary maternal role in my life. By my early adolescence, though, Sara had already made clear her designs on the job, vacillating between bossiness and over-nurturing during the games we'd play. At ten, when I lost Mom, I'd rushed up to manhood, bucking the coddling from Patricia and Sara and leaving it for Marc, who had conversely regressed from being my younger brother to being a baby brother, never again to leave the laps of the women in the family. Ten years later, when my father announced that he was moving back to Ste. Thérèse to look after my grandmother — and Marc said he was, in a way, going with him, taking his terrible French and his Francophone name to go and live with the Anglo-Montrealers, just forty minutes and a whole national identity away from Dad — I quickly found my orphan self-pity, ten years stale but no less potent. I ran into Sara's arms.

Her priority, back then, had been to nurse me out of the sudden resentment that I felt for my dad. She'd argued what she'd assumed would be his case, and did it with an elegance I doubt that he could have mustered: *It must be difficult for a widower father*, she'd imagined aloud. *Every child is going to cling to the mother who nursed him, with her softer voice and body. The way you hardened after losing her — he couldn't have known you'd still need him like this, this close, this immediate.* She'd soothed and mended, shrinking the distance for me between East Van and Ste. Thérèse, preserving the sanctity of my father-son relationship with him, now slightly abstracted, while cementing the mother-son relationship between herself and me.

"It is only because I love you so much, Daniel, that this worries me. It worries me to no end."

"Sara, fine. Thank you. But don't you — Can't you see how much better I am than six months ago? I told you, I'm still seeing the doctor every couple weeks. I am not ignoring the therapeutic, whatever, side of this. But you ... I know, Sara, I agree with you, but Christ — even ambulances burn fossil fuels."

She laughed at that, hugged me, and kissed me on both cheeks because I still felt more French-Canadian than Scottish.

○

Lonely Vancouver: in the eyes of the rest of the province just a citadel of faggots and Orientals, a lone and wilted copy of *Harper's* in a pile of old church bulletins. Waxy, cobblestoned Victoria buries itself deeper in its Anglophile pretensions in seemingly inverse proportion to the degree to which we in Vancouver embrace our place on the Pacific Rim, and the rest of the province would likely be just as happy to confederate with an independent Alberta built on oil money and resentment. The arrhythmic heart of this dissonance between the city and the province isn't the rollerblading and real estate speculation of the West End, nor the somehow-blond Koreans of Robson Street, nor the craven and earnest consumerism of Yaletown and Kitsilano, respectively. The title belongs, in fact, to my neighbourhood, a mosaic built, appropriately, by the kinds of people who work laying tile.

On Commercial Drive, short colourful buildings hug the skies and mountains closely to streets peopled by Italians, dykes, schizophrenics, hippies, yuppies, hipsters, Portuguese, West Indians, Ethiopians, yoga-enthusiasts, illegal drug-enthusiasts, Kurdish Marxists, right-wing Vietnamese, Salvadorans, Mexicans, Québecois migrant-vagrants finished picking Okanagan fruit for the season, sexily-clad high school girls somehow dressed both too old for their age (because they're kids) but too young for their station (because they're mothers), environmentalists, and all manner of leftists, foosball players, street musicians, and spoken-word poets.

In any other North American city — in any other part of Vancouver, really — each of those groups might have its own neighbourhood, or at the very least, a strip of one street or another staked out in a *lebensraum* turf war carried out over the course of romantic, Scorsesean, melting pot street battles; but there's another group of people on the Drive's census sheet, and it's they, I would argue, who make the mix possible.

In the New World, the clean-slate school of gentrification that passes a neighbourhood *in toto* from one ethno-clustering to the next ("These blocks used to be Irish, then Polish, and now it's all Filipinos," decries the embittered White Ethnic who once voted for Lester Pearson and now doesn't know what to think) works like an echo of the continent's Original Sin of conquest. My thinking is that since most of us are dealing in stolen goods — before this neighbourhood was Puerto Rican *or* Polish *or* Irish it was *Indian* (and not "Indian" like Fraser street, or Main at the south end, but Native, this-shit-used-to-be-and-still-is-*ours*, Indians)

— when we lose what we've got we've no moral recourse for redress. When a settler loses his neighbourhood, he's beset by the same love-and-war fairness that prevents the burglary victim from reporting the theft of a hot stereo.

The Drive is one of the few places in Canada outside Saskatchewan or Manitoba where urbanite settlers — and really, *Saskatchewan*, you can't honestly designate as "urban" a place whose staple harvest is legal — rub elbows daily with the descendants of the people that their predecessors tried to wipe out. In its non-rural, paved and pulsing setting, Commercial is one of the few arenas wherein pale- (and brown-from-elsewhere-) faces confront Natives not as semiotic pleas for tolerance or against littering, nor as beautiful artwork mounted in airports built on stolen land, but as neighbourhood people engaged in utterly banal chores and recreation, people who pet your dog as you pass them, or tell you to fuck off with that music, or ask you what time it is or who, in history's tiniest reparation, steal your parking space.

If there is any symbolism effected in this sometimes-easy back and forth, it's manifested in the understanding that hangs in the air on the Drive that no colonization is complete. No matter who comes to Commercial, the theoretical repulsion of that first wave of gentrification, testified to by the presence of the country's first peoples, is a fact that permeates the atmosphere with a message of forced, and now naturalized, sharing. Oh, and you can buy dream catchers almost anyplace.

All of this means that pregnant yuppy couples are moving in on blocks where old left-wingers like my landlord, Gary, bought houses in the seventies and eighties, and which are now presenting them with a material well-being for which they aren't ideologically prepared. Gary's Trotsky-ist reluctance to be a homeowner has excused without awk-wardness or even discussion the extra days I've taken at the beginning of many months to pay the modest sum asked in exchange for my gold-vein-mirrored suite in the old red house on Salsbury Street that Gary bought in 1983. The rent has, as testament to the enormity of my new obsession — photocopying medical journal articles or copying out by hand, Malcolm X-like, lines from the medical dictionary onto the yellow pages of legal pads — been more than a week late several times in past months. But in collecting it, Gary rarely offers more than a cynical and somewhat defeated ref-erence to his being a sell-out for being a landlord, making self-deprecating snips about property as theft, cribbed from a Proudhonist tradition of anarchism that otherwise doesn't jibe with his Trotskyism. He always asks how my day job is going; for some reason he seems sincerely to wonder how cleaning the unnoticed floors of underground parkades like some plebeian Sisyphus in rainpants and gumboots is *treat-ing* me. I think he's soothed by the thought of my manual labour, intoxicated by the proletarian romance that appeals only to people who've either never worked shit jobs or are holding out for revolution (two categories, unfortunately, that overlap all too often). He's not as impressed with my idiosyncratic dispatching of Marx to the frontiers of my psy-chic traumas. Once — when I'd told him I was learning about medical practices, materials, and technologies, using a less-than-orthodox reading of commodity fetishism as a means of purging myself of grief — he'd plunged his front teeth into his bottom lip, tightening his eyes and temples before moving onto the subject of the divots in his lawn.

Gary is a man whose greyness seeps and percolates from his hair down through to the colour of his face, clothing, and even his posture. He is wrapped, without fail, in a jean jacket peppered with sandy, faded patches that is constantly out of synch with denim pants always two shades lighter, or darker, than the coat. In the message he's left me, asking me if I'll come upstairs to see him about something, there's a greyness in his voice; there's a mumble, then some kind of whimper, then Gary's back on track — whenever I get the message, he says, never mind the time, just pop upstairs.

Once Robeson and his two moms (that's *two* moms to my none, he's got. Not precisely surplus value but it still seems pretty shitty, I think) have left, I pick the phone up from its cradle, dialing Gary, pressing the '7' harder, with my thumb, because it's jammed. Gary's phone, ringing thrice, can be heard through my open side window.

"Hello?"

"Gary? It's Daniel downstairs. Sorry to call so late — I don't know, your message said, you know — Is it too late to call?"

"No, Daniel. Hi. No, not at all, don't worry about it. I wanted you to call. Actually I needed you to call tonight. I'm — I've actually got to take off."

"Oh, sorry. Is this a bad time? You're out the door?"

"No, sorry. What I mean is I've got to take off tomorrow, so I needed you to call whatever time you could tonight. Are you, uh — What about you, is this a bad time for you?"

"No, not at all. I was just babysitting my nephew — "

"Robeson," he says, and adds, with a light but tragic kind of sarcasm: "The Stalinist."

"Yeah, right."

"No, so — You think you could come up here for two seconds, Daniel?"

"Oh, yeah. Totally. Just what — up back?"

"Yeah. The back door's open, so, you know — so just come on in. I'm in the living room."

Gary has shared with me, albeit in truncated, scatter-shot instalments, the story of his political life: How one of his first memories was standing — all of four years old, and shorter than the picket signs the fellow travelers around him carried — as part of an angry ring of protesters outside the grounds of the US embassy in Ottawa the night in 1953 that the Americans executed Julius and Ethel Rosenberg. His parents, Communist Party members raising Gary and his older sister Rosa in Toronto, had driven down from the city with the kids at the height of McCarthyite hysteria. My favourite of Gary's stories, the one that had me struggling hardest against cruel laughter, was the one about his sister's name.

The only vacation that Gary's parents ever took had been in Italy, and in the heavy romance of the foreign atmosphere, the nonchalance about the statues and the scooters nearly everywhere, they had been moved to the act that conceived their first child, whom they named with the Italian word meaning "red" — it had been a rare moment of whimsy, from what I had gathered of Gary's family life.

Only the other members of the Party, whenever they learned Rosa's name, assumed that she had been named for Rosa Luxemburg — an early, vocal left critic of Lenin and the Bolsheviks. His parents had explained and wearily re-explained the name's actual origins to suspicious party members so many times that by the time Gary was born they were not only going with an apolitical choice, but the blandest, least offensive one that they could think of.

As a teenager, Gary worked out his adolescent rebellion politically, renouncing his family's Stalinism (in fact his father, like many, had resigned from the Party in 1956 after Khrushchev's revelations, while his mother had retained her membership and gone on to what Gary described as "some prominence" in the anti-nuclear movement), attaching himself to the various strands of Trotskyism opposing the war in Vietnam and flirting with the Waffle movement inside the NDP. In 1972, a handful of them had formed the Labour Vanguard Group, or LVG. For several years, Gary had worked at the Party's nerve centre in English Montréal, editing and selling a bilingual Marxist weekly called *Militancy/La Militantisme*.

In late 1978, Gary's left cheek was caved in by an angry and patriotic fraternity boy from McGill – a "*Calice de Saint Esprit de tête carrée de marde*" as he was called by the elderly francophone who tended to Gary on the cold street corner under a thick spell of bemused, slightly condescending delight at having stumbled across a bespectacled Anglo willing to be shit-kicked for selling a newspaper demanding, in a bold-faced twenty-point type, "Independence for Quebec Now!" Nursing his wounds and determined to counter what the LVG had identified as the "growing Maoist influence among the East Indians" living on the country's West Coast, Gary joined the party's new branch in Vancouver. When dwindling membership forced the branch to shut down in 1994, and the rest of his comrades moved back either to Toronto or Montréal, Gary resigned from the party, exhausted, still subscribing to *Militancy/La Militantisme* (a biweekly now, and produced entirely in English) and sending nearly a quarter of every paycheque to the rump of the remaining LVG.

I say all this not only as a big fan of Gary, but also as a relatively unambiguous leftist myself (albeit with the proper aloofness, as befits my generation). I vote, usually without hesitation and with great from-the-left disappointment, for the NDP. I wouldn't ever cross a picket line, and at Sara's and Nicole's urging I've often joined demonstrations and earnest boycott efforts. But when Gary approached me once, in the backyard, complaining of the disintegration of his back issues and asking if I knew any secrets for preventing the discolouration of old newspaper (just a ploy, I think, to remind me of the paper's existence in the hope that I'd buy a subscription), it was all I could do not to tell him, "Gary, the journalism's *already* yellow." Red yellow journalism. Anywhere outside of Ireland or Ontario, you could call it Orange (though not really; in Canada, social democracy has already staked that colour as its own — fittingly, too yellow to be red).

When I come into his living room, Gary is seated on the floor, back up against the couch, staring with dead eyes at a blank spot on the wall in front of him, just underneath a framed photo of Thomas Sankara. There's half a bottle of red wine on the coffee table next to a book written by the General Secretary of the LVG, and when Gary realizes that I'm inside, he drains the glass he's drinking and refills it.

"Hi, Daniel. How are you?"

"I'm good, fine. You doing okay?"

"Uh — I've been better, actually, Daniel. Do you drink

wine?"

"I'm actually not supposed to."

"What do you mean? You're not religious, are you?"

"No, Gary, no," I say, laughing lightly. "No, I just – it's the antidepressants, actually. The medicine."

"Oh."

"Yeah, no. It's – I think that it's because alcohol is a depressant, and anyway, whenever I do drink, I get quite nauseous the next day."

"You should always follow doctor's orders, Daniel. I try."

"Yeah, no. For sure."

"A lot of this herbal stuff is quite reactionary." Gary is drunk. I notice that there is another, empty, wine bottle down against the side of the couch, resting on the hardwood floor between the TV with its vaguely ethnic cloth covering and the spot where Gary is sitting. "It's – a lot of it – it's this same sort of petty bourgeois, you know, very middle class kind of stuff. Dalai Lama."

I let "Dalai Lama" – used here as some sort of strange, expletive, Trotskyist punctuation – hang in the air before passing unchallenged.

"What's up, Gary? Are you okay? I got your message."

Gary gently exhaled a muted burp as he leaned forward, laying his once-more half-empty glass on the table next to the bottle and raising his eyebrows.

"Tomorrow morning," he said, "I'm leaving for Halifax for several weeks."

"Oh," I said. And then (idiotically, and knowing from the drunken tone that it couldn't possibly be for any good reason): "That sounds great."

Gary shook his head without closing his eyes.

"No, it won't be great. I'm going — family. It's — my brother has leukemia, Daniel. He's started chemotherapy, already lost all of his hair, his eyebrows. So I'm going back there because of that."

"Jesus," I said in a half-whisper, speeding past the obligatory thoughts of my mother at the mention of leukemia. "Jesus, Gary, I'm so sorry. I didn't — " I stop, questioning the appropriateness of this question, and then proceed with it anyway. "Gary, I didn't even know you *had* a brother."

"We haven't, ah — I haven't spoken to Travis since 1982, Daniel. Not since the Malvinas War."

I tried, unsuccessfully, to figure this riddle out on my own. Gary had a way of speaking in Trot history, using it as shorthand for his feelings. "Dalai Lama," "Social Democrat," "Moscow," "reformism," and "Kronstadt" were all words that he had used at various times, each symbolic of whole swathes of information, struggle, disagreement, and even, though he'd never approve of the term — too Hegel, too *early* Marx — zeitgeist. I knew by "Malvinas" that he meant the Falklands War, but I still didn't get what that had to do with his brother.

"Gary, I don't understand."

"Daniel," he said, looking up at my eyes for the first time since I arrived, "Would you please drink some wine with me?"

I went back to the kitchen to retrieve one of Gary's thick, Mexican clay mugs, and filled it halfway with the wine, which was from the Okanagan and tasted of black cherries (the kind that might be picked, I like to think, by some distant Francophone cousin of mine). The heat in my throat felt so good that I downed the glass in one pull, and followed Gary's pointing finger to the wine rack on the other side of the room for more.

"Travis and I," he said, "were on different sides of a split in the LVG around the issue of the Malvinas war. The Fourth International — let's just say that a lot of people were confused by that conflict. The Harrier-Vulcan faction — I should say, the tendency that Travis was a part of — believed that because the dictatorship in Argentina was so heatedly engaged with putting down a revolutionary movement in the country, that the international working class movement should lend its critical support to Thatcher's campaign."

"Right," I said, nodding, downing three-quarters of my glass of wine, relishing the heat and trying to ignore any thoughts about cancelling out the effects of a medication important enough for me to take against the wishes of my cousin, whom I loved dearly, all in order to offer solace to an incoherent, sectarian landlord.

"But you've got to realize," continued Gary, "As logical as that may or may not sound to you — I mean this is really a debate that we're seeing again today, in the so-called War on Terror, you know?"

I suppressed a smirk at Gary's unaffected insistence on the precision of political terminology. It was as though, if he forgot to qualify the War on Terror as "so-called," even now, in his living room rocking wine-soaked with fear, that I would think he was giving quarter to the oil barons. But Che had always insisted that we call things by their right names. Gary always made a point of refusing to use nicknames for politicians — he'd say "William Clinton," or "Anthony Blair" — because, he explained, they were class enemies, not old friends.

"I mean, to lend our political support to a military campaign launched by an imperial power," he continued, "that runs totally contrary to Leninist principles of internationalism. And so the party split. It was a messy, messy thing, and the numbers were close enough that both sides could claim that they had expelled the other."

"That must have been rough," I said, not sure about etiquette. What's the proper level of sympathy to express at the news of a quarter-century old split in an irrelevant political sect?

"I mean on May Day, in 1982, while my brother's faction was selling newspapers defending the British policy on the Malvinas, the English bombed Puerto Argentino, which the imperialists called Port Stanley, using Vulcan and Harrier planes. And so, as a derogation, after that, the tendency to which Travis belonged, we called them the Harrier-Vulcans."

"Was that, like, a *Star Trek* reference?"

"You know, that might have been a part of it, Daniel — as in, making the name more ridiculous. But we were, you know — and things just kept getting uglier for several years. They changed their name, and started selling a paper called *Real Militancy*. Their paper was only in English, and at the time of the Oka standoff, they dropped their support for Québec independence. Then we called them Anglo-chauvinists. The whole thing was awful. It just kept getting uglier. Back East there were full-on, physical confrontations. One guy got thrown down a flight of stairs."

"And you and Travis haven't spoken since?"

Gary shook his head, his face twisted into a half-sick,

half-wistful grimace.

"So — and he lives in Halifax?"

"Yeah."

"And what — did he call you — "

"No, I spoke to Rosa, my sister, earlier today. She's — apparently she's been living at his home in Halifax for nearly a month, looking after him. He's in very bad shape." He paused. "And I'm, you know, I'm going to need you to look after the house, you know — the plants and maybe the lawn. Turn the lights on every once in a while. Bring in my corporate newspapers. *Militancy* will probably only come once or twice while I'm gone."

Here, Gary started bawling, and I took his head down onto my shoulder and let it soak, spreading my fingers in the greyness of his thin, curling hair and eased the glasses off his face so that they wouldn't get bent.

"It's okay Gary," I said while I stroked and rocked him drunkenly on the couch, training my eye on the poster of Nelson Mandela and Fidel Castro tacked beside the bookshelf.

As Gary calmed himself, sniffing embarrassedly, he gruffly changed the subject, as he nearly always did, to my work life — the authentic, blue-collar drabness of which immensely excited him even now.

"How's work going?" he asked, but with the warmth of the wine and the raw honesty his breakdown had engendered, I refused to gear down.

"You know, Gary, the pressure washing — I don't know. It's not even how I spend most days."

"Are you still working on that medical thing?"

"Yeah, Gary. I am."

# III

"You like that? *Plasma.*"

"Plasma, huh?"

"That's right, Chief. Only the best these days."

"These flat-screens, I mean — yeah, they're gorgeous when you're staring straight on at them, right, but from the sides it's a bitch."

"Aw, fuck that. Truer picture, Chief. It's a truer picture," Ty said, repeating what the salesman had told him. He was doing his best to impress Colin, a Vancouver stand-up visiting LA for some middling gigs and who now squinted at the TV set, moving his large, shaved head slowly from left to right, shifting the weight from shoulder to shoulder. In Vancouver, they had been no more than casual acquaintances, but Colin's need of a place to stay and Ty's isolation in the new city had bonded them for the weekend. "I'm spoiling myself, dude," Ty mock-confessed. "Who knows how much longer I'll be pulling in cheques like I've been having?"

"It looks as though it'll be a while, at least, no? What's

going on with Sampson?"

"He's out of the coma, but it's still rough. Obviously he's not walking yet, or anything, although apparently the spinal cord wasn't severed anywhere. He had what's called spinal shock."

"Listen to you. Jesus, you're up on it, hey?"

"I guess so, homie. Got to be. It's my job were talking about, right?"

"I guess so."

For several weeks after Sampson's crash, *Army Brats* had been on hiatus, in reruns for the length of Sampson's three-week coma. When he pulled out of the coma — the doctors explained his progress as openly as they could to the television cameras, yet obliquely enough to meet the standards of privacy dictated by ethics and good taste — the producers finally moved ahead, calling a solemn press conference, and coaching Ty on humility.

"You aren't getting his job, you don't want his job," counselled Josh Stern, the show's youngest producer, gently holding the back of Ty's arm and looking ahead as he spoke. "Remember to emphasize the degree to which Al inspired you, made you want to become a comic. You're a place-holder, you're just keeping his seat warm — gush about him, okay? You aren't trying to replace him, you couldn't imagine trying to fill his shoes."

"Okay."

"This thing, handled incorrectly, and you come off like a ghoul. We all come off like ghouls. Do you know the orig-inal definition of a 'ghoul'? That's the one I'm talking about. Not just monsters, ghosts, but grave-robbers. We love Al and we wish him the best, and all this is temporary. Stopgap. And you're both Canadian. You're a natural place-holder here. Imitation is the sincerest — no. Don't say that. Just, you know, you're Canadian and he inspired you, leave it at that. And the temporariness. You're not a ghoul. Don't say it like *that*, you know, but you're not."

"Sure thing," he said.

Stern had booked a reception hall in one of LA's myriad chain hotels, distinguishable only by the names that hung on the buildings, in fonts and colours reminiscent of competitors'. At the front of the room was a long, white table with an equally white skirt, which would conceal Stern's tapping his toes fearfully whenever Ty answered questions from the reporters seated in the ten rows of chairs — seats laid out by some of the hotel's Chicano employees, while black and white female staff brought pitchers of water. There were only four seats behind the table, but the hotel had put out three full pitchers. The clear plastic containers were dewed with condensation and their bottoms stained the white cloth with darkening circles of wet, grey translucence, circles that crept out slowly, like continents.

"I want to thank everyone for coming out here today," said Josh, starting the press conference from behind the podium, no water, just him looking tall, thin, and appropriate in a perfect suit. He was a handsome man, tanned skin and eyelashes like the fringe of an Oriental rug, magnetic, with a suitably solemn voice. "My name is Joshua Stern and I'm one of the executive producers of *Army Brats* and I've had the very great honour and pleasure of working beside Al for several years now, and they've been the most rewarding of my career." As he spoke, entertainment reporters fingered their microphones while those from legitimate news pounded their keypads and photographers scaled the room. "Al has recently recovered from the initial coma which set in after his terrible accident, and that is very good news. Nevertheless, and while I'm proud of the top-notch care that Bratspack is providing for our dear friend and colleague, this is still a very difficult and serious situation, and our thoughts, as well as our prayers, are with Al at this time, and they're also with his wife, Lynn, his daughter Felicity, and his son Sasha.

"Al is one of those rare individuals who manages to be both a star as well as a member of a team. In this sense he has always reminded us of his fellow countryman, Steve Nash, of whom Al is a devoted fan — much to the chagrin of the Lakers fans he works with." Those assembled responded with appropriately soft smiles. "It's in Al's capacity as a member of a team, I think, that the difficulty of what to do with the show — the project he loves so much — while he is incapacitated becomes so fraught with difficult decisions. After long consideration, and after having postponed production of this season's episodes for the duration of Al's coma, it has been decided that the show must continue, and that too many people's livelihoods are affected for production to be canceled this season. I assure you that it is with great reluctance that we move into the booths to record episodes without our Al. No one could ever, ever in a million years, take his place...."

The hermitic Zavarise was next, wearing a loose and uncomfortable button-down, his thick, grey hair pulled back into a ponytail, fingers bothering a craggy goatee. He wore a pinky ring made of onyx, the black standing out against the pale pinkness of his fingers, their skin betraying every skeletal dimension underneath.

At 57, Zavarise's age was hard to guess, softened at the edges. He had managed to stay slim, unlike most poor people who find themselves suddenly flush with untold wealth, but a wide variety of smokes had textured his skin and voice. A long scar ran down from the corner of Zavarise's left eye, splashing the space to his earlobe with a grainy patch left over from Vietnam-era street wars with the police. Even after the borderless success of *Army Brats*, Zavarise had continued to publish his syndicated comic strip, *Dopes*, about the misadventures of three burnouts consistently dumbfounding the neighbourhood narcs. He frequently donated his artwork to committees and organizations opposed to police brutality.

"Al Sampson is the most talented comic actor, you know, just performer that I've ever worked with, ever seen, man," Zavarise had gushed, not referring to Ty, or even looking at him, the whole time that he spoke. "Al brought my characters to life, you know. He was — he's tapped in to the transcendental capacities of humour, the sublime potential of satire. The legendary Zero Mostel once said that, quote, the freedom of any society varies proportionately with the volume of its laughter, unquote. I believe that that's true, and I believe that, in line with that thinking, Al knows more about freedom than any politician or army general anywhere in the world.

"He brought my characters to life, and I have no doubt that he'll, you know, fight to pull himself through this, and we'll all be there waiting for him when he does. I also want to share my love and support with Al's wife, Lynn, and his children, and just, you know emphasize how much we're pulling for Al's quick recovery."

When Ty had spoken, he had done so in line with the instructions that he'd been given, speaking shortly, self-effacingly.

"I just can't begin to describe how, you know, *insane* it is to think of me even trying to fill Mr. Sampson's — Al — I feel like I can call him Al, you know, back home, we all really feel like Al's a hometown boy, right, and so, it's like he's family or a friend. Al was a total, like, huge influence for me, and he's the reason that I'm in comedy today, you know, and I'm just like — think of me as a bookmark. I'm just holding his place until he's ready to get back here." Then, thinking that the last sentence may have sounded too jocular, too command-like, Ty softened his conclusion. "I just want to see him back here as soon as possible." *So that I can go back to being unemployed*, he would have said if they'd let him be funny. He would have been far more eloquent if they would have let him be funny.

○

Several days after the press conference, Ty drove to work from the apartment that the show was putting him up in, eager to meet his castmates at his first read-through. Monday mornings, the cast would meet to read the script for the new episode in the presence of Stern, whomever was directing the episode in question, one or two animators (though the bulk of the show's animation work was done in South Korea) as well as the writers themselves, clad in ironic T-shirts and thick plastic glasses, careful stubble giving the appearance of spontaneity and a disregard for maintenance.

After the read-through, the writers went back to their work with notes from the directors and voice actors, and even the animators. By Tuesday, the final revisions to the scripts were ready, and as the writers turned to drafting the material for the next Monday's read-through, the actors moved into the booths. Animators would watch the actors' facial expressions, suggest notes to match up the performances with pre-existing notions about how the episode would look, and by Thursday evening, most of the vocals would have been recorded.

For his first Monday, Ty arrived in the long, board-room-style office a few minutes early, and joined some of the writers milling about the coffee and snacks laid out on a small table at the side of the room. One by one, the cast members entered the office in sweatpants, ballcaps pulled low, the women with hair in lazy ponytails, men three or four days unshaven. Sergeant Brats's wife and children were voiced by a single performer, the four-foot-eleven-inch Pamela Fried. His General and his Pastor were Hal Kennedy, a recovering alcoholic and Second City mainstay — an old friend of Sampson's from the Chicago days. His military underlings were played by Larry Roth, a part-time Shakespearean, and Sammy Mallick, a Palestinian-American live-action TV actor who normally played Italians. The female army Captain and his children's schoolfriends were all Debbie Hunting, whose WASPy name belied the Greek blood that granted her the pronounced nose and hips, the breasts that Ty stared at throughout the read-through. As they filed in, so did the verbal detritus of early workweek small talk. Roth laughed hoarsely and made his way over to the snack table, front teeth unspooling a Danish from its nucleus. Roth smiled at Ty and gave him a wink as he swallowed the pastry nearly whole. None of the others bothered to say a thing.

"Happy Monday, everybody," announced Josh, as he arrived with the episode director, Tim White, prompting a deluge of smart-ass replies. From the writers, the rejoinders were current affairs-based — "Not a happy Monday for so-and-so," referring to some scandal elucidated on some blog. From the actors, the responses were character-based, delivered in varied accents and tonal experimentations.

"First piece of business today," continued Josh, "is that I want everybody to welcome Tyler Bergen from Vancouver, Canada. Tyler, as you guys know, is the sound-alike for Al while he's in — while he's getting better. Tyler is, um — Tyler's an impressionist, a very accomplished impressionist — "

"Worked with Monet," deadpanned one of the writers, to mild giggles.

"What else? He is a touring stand-up comic, done some commercials, I think, some national spots up in Canada, yeah Tyler?"

"Yup."

"Am I missing anything?"

"Nope, not really. I mean, JFL, Aspen. I did a *Comedy Now*."

"Right, sure. Just For Laughs, Aspen. So, yeah — please welcome Tyler Bergen everybody."

A short smattering of applause followed, during which his new co-workers looked at Ty and offered smiles of varying admixtures of sincerity, condescension, and suspicion.

"Is there any news about Al from the weekend, Josh?" asked Debbie, looking concerned. "When will he be back?"

Ty tried not to look stung when buxom, Grecian Debbie's only response to his introduction was to ask, by implication, how long he'd be working there. Instead, he watched her chest rise and fall as she shared her deep feelings for Al Sampson, her hopes for his speedy recovery.

Later in the day, Ty made his way down to the soaring, neon-lit cafeteria, with its Starbucks brand beans and real, zinging Thai food served with ice cream scoops. Across the room, and holding a small espresso cup between his fingers, Josh raised his eyebrows, then his hand, and moved to join Ty as he pushed his black plastic tray along the stainless metallic counter it was meant to match.

"How'd it go today, Tyler?"

"Pretty good, man, thanks. How are you doing?"

"Oh, I'm not too bad, Tyler. Just doing what I'm normally doing, running around trying to catch my own tail." Josh smiled, tanned and pleasant, finishing his coffee and putting it onto the heated glass casing on the counter above the entrées. He wasn't paying attention to the disgruntled, hair-netted tsks this elicited from behind the counter, behind a black apron. "But everything was cool, everybody, I mean?"

"Yeah, I think so."

"Anyway, it was good of you to downplay your credits today at the read-through."

"What do you mean?" Ty had been honest about his credits, neither inflating them nor whispering them into his chest, pretending they weren't there, that they weren't his.

"Well, I probably should have had a chat with you earlier about this, I guess, but I'm sure you were probably able to pick up on it today, whatever, the *vibe*." Nervous giggle.

"There was a pretty strong feeling from a lot of the cast that things got moved along too quickly, you know. That we should be waiting for Al, you know, a bit longer before thinking about a replacement, no matter how short-term."

Ty didn't respond, but neither did he look away. He stared, blankly, at Josh, before reaching into his pocket to pay for his pad Thai. It would be another week before payroll set up his account at the cafeteria.

"I'm sure I don't have to tell you," Josh continued, "that Al's a pretty special guy, you know, and he's pretty — people around here are pretty devoted to him. And I just wanted to make sure that you weren't bearing any of the brunt of, you know, resentment that some folks may have towards the higher-ups."

Josh waited for something from Ty. Then:

"Anything like that, Tyler?"

"No, I mean, nothing — No."

"Good. I mean good, you know, that's good. And I suppose, um, that in the interest of full disclosure — I mean this is show business, I'm sure you aren't expecting full disclosure from anyone. And that's probably best."

Ty laughed. "Tell me about it. Totally."

"Right. But it's important for me that, you know — in the interest of being upfront, I should just tell you that I spoke against moving ahead this quick, okay, and so some of the cast are mad at me, because they — and you know, to an extent they were right, I suppose — but they identified me as sharing their sentiments on this and then moving ahead anyway. I'm sure you can imagine that we're all in sort of a shitty situation with this stuff. Al's family, you know?"

"What happened to his family?"

"Sorry?"

"Al's family?"

"No, sorry, I meant like, 'Al *is* family.'"

"Oh."

"And I just want to make sure that you don't get guilted around on this, or that you're made to feel bad about something that, you know, it isn't your fault. You're just doing your job."

"Yeah, I know. I don't feel bad. I mean, I feel like it's awful that Al has got to be in the hospital –"

"Right."

"But, you know. So no worries, man, I'm guilt-free."

"Good." Josh clasped Ty's shoulder for a moment longer, nodding. "Good."

# IV

Before descending into the basement of the Biomedical Library, I always check my email on the computers on the main floor, where there are other people and ambient light from outside. This time, my father had sent me a note in French that I couldn't read — the unilingual browser I was using had no capacity for his grave and acute accents, and so the composition was scrambled. Besides that, there was only one other new message, from Gary, in my Hotmail account. It had been three weeks or so since he'd left for the East Coast, and he'd affixed the subject line "Working all the Engels" to his letter. So I now know he has a brother, a brother with cancer, as well as a sense of irony, even possibly a sense of humour. Where was it all coming from?

Dear Daniel,

Hope everything is okay at the house and with you. Been a pretty crazy few weeks. I was here two days before I slept. Rosa is holding down Travis's place, and I'm staying with her. I brought Engels's

"The Origins of the Family" for airplane reading. How do you like that? I didn't even do it on purpose.

We spend a few hours every day at the hospital with my brother. We went out to Peggy's Cove, which I hadn't seen in thirty years, then drove out to Lunenburg to see the Bluenose. Halifax is truly a beautiful place. The Acadians and the Mi'kmaq seem to be reasserting their presence here too. That's pretty good.

Please make sure that you water the plants once a week, but most important is to make sure you bring the papers in off the porch every day. Otherwise people will know I'm not home. Take in the mail from the box every couple days as well. Also help yourself to any food in the fridge. I may end up being here a bit longer than I had initially expected. No use anything going bad.

The weather in Halifax is pretty okay. The city's a lot quieter than Vancouver. Just try to imagine a Tim Hortons substituted for every Starbucks and you'll get the idea of what service industry capitalism out here looks like.

Seeing Travis was one of the hardest and easiest things I have ever done. Ever had to do, I should probably say. Twenty years of estrangement becomes very thin, it narrows, but it's sharp, still, and it cuts every sentence we share, essentially. Rosa's presence has helped. I think that, in a way, she's jealous that, as it turned out, I rather than she was a match for the transplant. Sorry, I should explain, they did a blood test, just in case Travis needs a bone marrow transfusion later on, if anything comes back after remission. They figured I ought to do the test while I was out here. His leukemia is acute, and so the chances are fairly good (meaning bad, meaning terrible) that I'll have to come back in a few months for another procedure. I'm the match for Travis. Would I be a sentimental philistine if I said I knew, from the time Rosa first called me in Vancouver, that I would be? I felt it, something between my brother and me. Not dialectical, but certainly antagonism. Struggle.

They said before the transplant can take place, if it does, I'll need to up my levels of iron, which will take a couple of weeks, so they'll get me on supplements, which I'd be taking for a few weeks after the procedure, too. I told them I thought we were getting ahead of ourselves. I bring it up because my brother had a pretty good line. He told them that any transplant better be carried out by a member of the ironworkers' union, because he didn't want the blood to scab.

Take care,
Gary


I closed the browser and took in the room before setting to work, looking at the dozen or so researchers and doctors with whom I was sharing the space, people at the centre and on the fringes of healing, some men and more women, all looking down at their notes or their books, even the ones speaking mutedly to the librarians kept their chins tucked and eyes bowed. I don't need to be here — with the advent of the Internet, its easily navigable medical databases and indexes, and with online medical dictionaries far more recent and up-to-date than the old, taped, torn, and dusty second-hand job I'd been using with its cover in a now-extinct version of mauve, I probably don't even have to leave my basement suite in order to pursue my anaesthetizing work. Everything could be accomplished hunched over the small space by the bookshelf in the living room that I've set aside for the old computer Nicole gave me. Instead, I wake up mornings and take the bus to the Biomedical branch of the UBC library, a ritual that gives the whole enterprise at least the flavour of a real job, and in so doing takes away some of the stink of insanity that hangs around the project. The Biomedical Library is on the second floor of an old building tucked into a smallish corner of the vast grounds of Vancouver General Hospital, past the Thai delicacies on Cambie Street and before the Jewish delicatessens on Oak. Across the street is an optimistic, colourful mural painted in tribute to a money-raising cancer research effort that is likely long-since finished and long-since failed. I sit in the library at least five or six hours a day, in the shadow of the building wherein my mother got better before she died, and use a friend's student log-in number and library card to get at the myriad resources there for those who can afford a tuition beyond the reach of a pressure-washer.

I should say that before my research project started, I did wash enough parking lot floors to pay for two years' worth of grazing the arts courses on offer at Langara College, whose campus sits nestled at the precise East/West axis between the Punjabi Market and a public golf course where working class Vancouver turns rich. Mine was a lazing, soft-focused course of study, during which I nevertheless became engaged enough to feel disgust at the airy, existential world-views of my classmates in English Literature courses while at the same time growing jealous and increasingly admiring of the cold, detached placidity of the Marxist professors who taught me History and Political Science. I began enviously referring to their calm dialectical materialism as *delectable* materialism, vowing to any of my friends who would listen (not many, granted) that I would overhaul my obscurant, Hegelian, spiritual, and sentimental intellectual upbringing with an eye to a philosophy that favoured real life, from the ground up. Things that had weight, that could be held in the hand (and, in *particularly* dialectical circumstances, thrown at cops).

Later on, as the outlines of my mental illness took shape, it would become obvious why I would take to a phi-losophy that spurned the ethereal, thought-based world in favour of materialism. But I didn't know anything back then, and so I recreated a pattern as old as psychoanalysis itself: ignorant of how the brain works, I blamed my prob-lems on a girl.

Specifically, in this case, my short-term girlfriend at the time — a pretty English student named Louisa. Louisa was a thin, dark-haired, scarf-wearing waif who felt she *understood* Margaret Laurence and who started crying when I told her that I had never dreamed of my mother, not *once* that I could remember, since she'd died.

Through her tears — to which I responded with a sort of shocked lack of understanding, a bewildered and nearly angry confusion — she tried to explain her dismay, reaching out to touch my face but drawing back, frightened, before making contact.

"That's a more profound orphaning than her physical loss, Daniel. How could she be so absent from your *soul*?"

I let Louisa's airy condescension take the rap for driving me away from the arts and into the arms of cool-headed historical materialism; in retrospect, though, there's another reason for my hostility to literature, and it has something to do with the quasi-illiteracy that came by way of obsessive-compulsive disorder. It was a confused, trembling anger born from sitting in a classroom discussing achingly brilliant books written sometimes by prodigies, by kids who had become authors earlier in life than I had discovered the *name* of the sickness that kept me from maintaining unbroken or even functional concentration throughout a single chapter of their or anyone else's novels.

Apparently one out of every forty people in Canada is supposed to have obsessive-compulsive disorder, which means that on every six full-load runs of a typical elevator, there will ostensibly be two or three of us, obsessing and compulsing, jangling our keys a specific number of times or saying a particular prayer in order to keep the rest of you from plummeting, along with us, down the shaft. (By the way: *You're welcome*, assholes.)

There are different permutations of OCD, and the primary obsessions subset of the disorder, mine, is as easy as it is terrible to describe. Essentially, some alchemical brew of anxiety, maybe misfiring synapses, maybe a serotonin drought in the brain, maybe trauma, conspire to produce and (this is essential) *infinitely reproduce* the most horrifying ideas and images of which the sufferer can conceive.

Doctors generally assign the obsession to one of three categories: *blasphemy* (say, for instance, the neverending image of wrapping beer-baked shanks of ham with pages torn from the Qur'an); *violence* (perhaps the imagined and re-imagined thud of a rock dropped into a sleeping baby's crib); and *sexual misconduct* (so, like, a constantly re-broadcast picture of you slipping a phallus up underneath an old man's oxygen mask). Some sufferers are lucky enough to keep their tormenting daydreams safely inside one of the three categories — others move into the borderlands, picking up combinations of two, sometimes all three.

The particular cruelty of the disorder is its unwholesome irony: only if you love children will you be obsessed and haunted by thoughts of their molestation; only if you want nothing more than to take care of old ladies will you be ceaselessly tormented by thoughts of lighting them on fire.

Take the ham-wrapping — for a Christian or an atheist, the idea is a brow-furrowing curiosity or an irrelevant bother at best, no crisis of faith, no worry about damnation, and easily forgotten. It takes a Muslim's devotion to God's law to find the thing a horror, but that's not the way she feels about it as it happens. All she feels is the sacrilege and the God-hatred pounding at the backs of her eyes every second of the day, drowning the sublimation of prayer, darkness running interference between herself and Him.

The searing guilt wrought by the thoughts, of which the thinker is the only victim, often translates into physical or mental rituals meant to ward off the bad feelings or absolve the imagined transgressions. These arbitrary compulsions, of course, don't help at all in the medium- or long-term and, in fact, end by making things only more nightmarish and infinitely worse. But just like the hawkish liberal rooting for bombing raids to liberate women on the other side of the world, the obsessive-compulsive continues to make a situation he doesn't understand that much worse by trying to fix it.

I've had the disorder since childhood, though of course I didn't know I had it; all I knew was that I was, as Mom called me, a "worry wart," with a tendency to introspection that would blossom over time into a howling McCarthyite witch-hunt that never receded. The first stirrings announced themselves with the bifurcation of my five-year-old mind into eternal prosecution and defence, sitting at the foot of the bed across the room from Marc's: *I hate you, God.* No! I don't! *Yes, I do. I hate you, God.* No!

When the swollen testicles and intellectual scepticism of adolescence set in, the thoughts shifted from religion to sex and violence (about four years after the release of the Boogie Down Productions album of the same name). Marbled through every daydream or meditation were pictures of stabbing and slitting, fondling and violating. My mind's eye became blood-spattered.

Hence, my hostility to English class. When the inside of your head is the only unsafe place in the world, the imaginative plane of fiction loses lustre. The creativity demanded by the novel's receiver — the COD demanded for the transmission of literature — sets the already hyperactive mind into overdrive, leaving the actual work behind and visiting whatever horrors terrify the reader most with a breakneck, relentless speed that demands, after a while, literary surrender followed by the soft mental deafness of the television. Picking through the phrases and sentences of a piece of fiction was like eating a meal that I was certain had broken glass in it — I started to ignore the flavours and the smells as I moved every bite around my mouth looking for it, using my teeth as a sift and sucking at air.

With the study of history, I could strip-mine a text or tract, scan for facts and extrapolate opinions, coasting, in seminars, for hours-long discussions based on just a few paragraphs worth of reading. Literature, though, called for such a delicate attention to cadence — commas and semicolons and metre, ideas and winks and thoughts hidden and buried and wrapped, distorted and disguised. I grew so angrily helpless in the face of it, so paralyzingly envious of the celebrated young novelists who'd clearly spent early adulthood swallowing millennia of knowledge with a discipline I needed prescription drugs to achieve, that I had washed my hands of the enterprise and stopped trying to catch up.

One of the chief pleasures that I drew from my treatment later on was the ability to move back into a reading chair, tilting the lampshade to soak pages with light. I read mostly at home because I was shy about what I was taking in, all the books you're supposed to read as a teenager and that wear as slight embarrassments after that; what can a twenty-six year old really take from *The Catcher in the Rye*? If anybody saw me reading *Brave New World*, I thought, they would assume that I'd dropped out of high school.

But I relished it — I moved through touchstones of the post-pubescent literary, gathering up the reference points that all the English majors had brought to those once-terrifying seminars.

The reading that had been such a hallmark of my slow crawl to health culminated, I guess, in my research, adapting itself to a far different plane. The Biomedical Library is a different thing entirely — there are no *stories* here, really, no culture-shaping narratives. The space too is different, less misty-eyed; the usual patronizing library posters promoting literacy have been replaced by more utilitarian, still-patronizing notices delineating rules that one wouldn't imagine would have to be explained to those capable of wrapping their heads around medical theory and statistics. One sign next to the phone, for instance, reads, "Please do not write on walls. Use scrap paper provided." Roughly every six inches is some variant of: "No eating or drinking in the Biomedical Library." These signs are rendered in varying degrees of good and bad cop, and run the gamut from polite pleases and thanks to vulgar, simple pictures of insects and hamburgers with Xs crossed through them. By deductive reasoning, I had long since determined that at one point in time, the Biomedical Library must have had problems with either food, bugs, or both. See? *This* is the quality of a mind wasted on parking lots.

Within a few weeks of starting my research, days spent in the library grew from once to twice a week, soon thrice and then four times. I stopped noticing the details, author names like Berkowitz's, and began simply to breathe in the wonderful, sterile numbness that came from reducing human suffering — *my* suffering — to nothing more than Platonic shadows bounced off the tools used by doctors to ease it.

To reach that sort of calm, though, took time. On research days, I would go downstairs to the "Current Journals" section, where actual offerings were not current, but where there was a whirring, airy silence and stillness ensured by the windowless inhospitality of the space. Cracks were visible along the painted sides of the piping that ran through the room at the same height as the low squares of neon that kept it lit. I perused the shelves at random, *au hazard*, searching for the least human, most machine-oriented journal titles available, ones that best obscured highly emotional experiences with illness and pain in favour of hospital mechanics. These would help me to do the same with mine. Occasionally, though, the opposite might present itself, and I would be tragically drawn in by the horrifying antithesis of what I was searching for. Such was the case with a journal called *Trauma Quarterly*, which I found on my first day in the library.

With morbid curiosity, I ran my finger along the spine of bound volumes 6-7 of *Trauma Quarterly*. It's just like *Gentlemen's Quarterly*, I told myself, only instead of being about gentlemen, *it's about fucking trauma*. These were stacked next to the placidly and comfortingly titled copies of *Vox Sanguinis*. Volumes 6-7 of *TQ*, I noted, were from 1989/90-90/91, starting when I was nine years old and had a mom, and had never been to California. By the time volume 7 was finished, I had been to Disneyland, was eleven, and — single-parent semantics aside — orphaned.

The subject headings in *Trauma Quarterly* were, I guess, to be expected: "Penetrating wounds of the extremities"; "Management of the cocaine-intoxicated trauma patient" (wouldn't '89-'91 have been a little late — or now, again, *early* — to catch the coke boom?); "Penetrating wounds of the spine"; "Stab wounds of the back and flank"; "Penetrating wounds of the neck." It occurred to me that *Trauma Quarterly* has, likely, several paid staff whose full-time job it is to work in a place called *Trauma Quarterly*, deciding which anatomical region's penetrating wounds would be showcased in which season.

Once *Trauma Quarterly* had lived up to its name with such gusto, leaving me bracing myself against an onslaught of unwelcome thoughts (disturbing images of penetrating wounds, always me doing the stabbing, always a loved one wounded), I chided myself for forgetting the thrust of the enterprise, reminding myself to keep it technical and not to let my anthropocentric curiosity get the better of me. I tried to stay focused while surveying the corridors of shelving downstairs, where I found journals like *Infectious Diseases in Clinical Practice* along with the bluntly titled *Injury*. Instead of caving again, I picked up one of their neighbours — *Journal of Clinical Ultrasound*, number 9, from November/December 1993. So I'm fat and thirteen again, the good David Berkowitz has recently penned his opus for the Catholics, Bill Clinton has been president for almost a year, and the Progressive Conservative Party of Canada has just crumpled and imploded — and I make my way over to the study carrels with their pull-string mini-neon lights. Any defacement of these carrels by vandals bored with their studies is ossified, fossilized, emphasizing less that these areas are used by human beings and more simply that they haven't been used in years. On one, there is a bumper sticker for the ancient radio station "LG73," the last place ever to have Top 40 on an AM frequency in Vancouver (the station has undergone several new manifestations, mandates, and sets of call-letters since the time when I was a kid and my father won beach towels and baseball tickets in a dial-in contest to what was then called the LG Morning Zoo). On another carrel was a muted exchange in ballpoint pen: A wavy smiley face next to the inscription "I am a macrophage," to which someone had responded: "A true phagocyte!"

I sat down to pore over the *Journal of Clinical Ultrasound* and found a whole host of articles which seemed, to me, entirely antiseptic and inhuman and therefore perfectly suited to my enterprise. Doctors Fitzgerald and Yock, for instance, had penned a piece called, "Mechanisms and Outcomes of Angioplasty and Atherectomy Assessed by Intravascular Ultrasound Imaging." I breathed in deeply, smiling, until my eyes traveled downpage to the article written by Shmulewitz, Teefey, and Robinson: "Factors Affecting Image Quality [*fine so far*] and Diagnostic Efficacy [*nice, yes*] in Abdominal Sonography [*perfect...*]: A prospective study of 140 patients." Fuck! My discovery here, of humans, was fearful and disappointing. As though I were Dr. Zaius from *Planet of the Apes*, my whole psychological sturdiness, in this endeavour, pivoted on the absence of human folk.

Some tiny echo of the same curiosity that led me to flip through *Trauma Quarterly*, made me turn to Shmulewitz et al.'s work on page 624, and take a paragraph at random:

> The patient was generally studied in the supine position. When necessary, the patient was asked to change position obliquely toward the contralateral side.

I exhaled ecstatically, with a small, tight smile pulling at the edges of my mouth as I ran my knuckles along the page. Something about that supine, oblique patient was so soothing and removed. I sat and lost myself in the opaqueness of the prose, filtering pain and sickness through polysyllables and getting further from it the deeper down I went.

○

"Sara? It's me, Daniel."

"Hi, honey. How are you?"

"Good, I'm good. I, uh — I found a story today that I thought you'd find funny."

"Oh yeah?"

"Yeah, I was — I was looking into some of the new technology around these wheelchairs for quadriplegics. You remember, like that straw that Christopher Reeve used to blow into?"

"Right, yeah, I remember that, Daniel. Oh, shit — Daniel, can you hold on just a second?"

"Sure." I waited for a few seconds, not interested in decoding the muffled sounds of Sara's treble clef voice as it called out after Robeson. At moments such as these, all psychic energies went into containing the chest-spreading guilt that was the corollary of my ill will towards that spoiled little two-mothered shit. You tell me what kind of prick begrudges a child his mothers?

"Daniel?"

"Yup."

"Sorry about that, honey. I heard a crash in Robeson's room — he knocked over that small bookshelf — you remember the one that Marc built?"

"Sure," I said, laughing. My brother had been thirteen years old when Robeson was born, and had built a little book-and-toy-shelf for him in wood shop in Grade Eight as a present. What Marc had forgotten in the process was to request non-toxic paint for the job. Instead, Sara had had to store the poisonous gift until Robeson was old enough to be trusted not to chew the corners. Marc — by the time he built it, already tall, with a deep voice and a forehead covered in acne — had been so angry at his mistake that he had kicked a hole into the wall of our hallway at home, which my dad took three years to fix. After he'd sanded down the area where the hole had been, I teased him and my brother by reminding them to paint it over with non-toxic paint.

"So what's going on with Christopher Reeve? I thought he passed away."

"No, yeah. He did. I just meant, like, you know that technology that he used? I was reading about that stuff, and like the innovations on that stuff. That's all."

"Oh."

"Anyhow, I came across this story, doing a Google search, and I came across this story about this one quadri-plegic guy, this totally sleazy-type kind of guy, and he's par-alyzed from the neck down by this car accident. And as you're reading through the piece he reveals that the way he got in the accident was because he was leering at these girls as he drove past a high school — he saw this one girl in shorts and he rammed into a streetlight pole. It was hilari-ous. I forwarded it to you."

She was silent.

"Sara?"

"Daniel, that's *awful*."

Shamed nausea shot into my stomach at the same time

as sick heat shot into my ears.

"What would make you think that I would find a story like that funny, Daniel? What kind of person do you — What did *you* find funny about that story?"

"I don't know," I said quickly, low-voiced. "I'm sorry."

"No, Daniel, tell me."

"No, nothing. I'm sorry."

She: loud, sad exhalation.

"I just thought — I'm sorry. I thought the guy was, like, being a pig and then he got fucked up, but, you know — No, it's awful. I'm really ashamed."

"Fine."

"Um, Sara — is Robeson okay?"

"Yeah, he's fine. I told you it was just the bookshelf."

"No, I mean, from last time he was over here. The *Clockwork Orange* thing."

"Oh, he's fine. He had a nightmare or two, and he asked to sleep with us a few times after that. I let him have a cuddle and fall asleep, but then carried him back to bed. It's just too tough for Nicole, right, because she just hasn't been sleeping well."

"The *Turtledoves* stuff?"

"Yeah, it's this pastor. He's apparently, for the past few elections, he's tried and failed to get the nomination from his riding association. Nicole's been in contact with one of the NDP people out there, this incredible Sikh woman, Gurmit Sihota — she's been so good and so much help for us — and anyhow, Gurmit thinks that this pastor — "

"What's his name?"

"Roger Gerry. Anyhow, Gurmit thinks that he's going to try to use this book-banning thing to build up enough, you know — So he can run again next time, I guess."

"Jesus."

"This woman, Gurmit — I don't know how the NDP, with all its fuck-ups, has managed to hold on to a gem like her."

"No shit."

"And — I don't know. I guess I just wish, you know — you remember how our friend Sheila wanted to do the illustrations for the book, before Nicole decided to illustrate it herself?"

"I think I remember you saying that."

"Well, I just find myself wishing we had let her. It's like — I think that Nicole feels as though she, alone, bears all the responsibility for this book. And in a way, you know, she knows I'm there for her, but it *is* her book. And she's totally alone in that. And I just feel like if Sheila had been involved, you know — I don't know."

"I'm so sorry, Sara."

"She's just — "

"Sheila?"

"Nicole. She's just been up all hours of the night, you know," Sara's voice dropped in to a whisper. "I'm finding hair all over her pillow and in the shower and in her brush. And she's just eating and eating. She is just falling apart with this stuff."

○

"What do you have coming out?" I asked, watching the grilled metal belt turning underneath the heat of the pizza oven, two of the rounded, golden, sesame seed-covered crusts barely visible as they moved slowly into readiness.

"Potato and Sweet Veggie," he said in a thick Kurdish accent, without looking up, re-organizing the full-pies, half-pies, and individual slices with metal tongs in order to maximize space under the heat lamps.

"I'll just have the Pesto and — is that Spicy Chicken?"

"No — that's Spicy Artichoke."

"Spicy Artichoke?"

"Yes."

"Is there onions on it?"

"Yes."

"I'll just have the Pesto and a Cheese and Garlic."

Many years from now, well-fed anthropologists studying Vancouver at the turn of the twenty-first century will explore the ways in which a whole human substratum like me — unmarried men earning significantly less than ten thousand dollars a year — survived by dint of the city's wholly unique Buck-a-Slice economy. Denny — a former drug dealer in his fifties with whom I often stop to speak when I see him on his late-night, anti-war postering runs on the Drive — has a theory that the cash-only, impossible-to-audit, Buck-a-Slice industry grows out of Vancouver's throbbing, teeming marijuana economy. *How else*," he posits, "*can I get a slice of pizza with four artichoke hearts and six chunks of chicken for a dollar and a half?*" If Denny's right, then the city's sundry, semi-generic pizza places are a far better cover than the Vietnamese Internet café I'd once visited on Kingsway, where two computers (one broken) were plugged in not ten feet from a massive, round white table surrounded by card players under an opaque shell of smoke. When first he advanced this theory to me, I met it with suspicion, to which

Denny responded: "The BC economy is all chiaroscuro, Daniel. Illegal marijuana here is like if Alberta criminalized oil."

Coming out of the shop with the slice of Pesto folded in my hand, I noticed a young kid with a stringy moustache bending back the fingers on his girlfriend's hand — he spoke to her through gritted teeth, and she was crying. I stood and watched for a second, taking the first hot bite of my buck-slice without my eyes leaving him.

On the questionnaires used by doctors to determine if a prospective patient has OCD, many of the questions aim at discovering an overworked and unreasonable sense of re-sponsibility — one of the typical inquiries asks the form-filler to either agree or disagree with the statement that "to not prevent something bad from happening is as bad as doing it on purpose." The obsessive-compulsive generally agrees that it is.

One of my worst fears in this vein is that a woman might be raped or beaten in a situation where, had I been vigilant enough, I could have protected her. I once went crazy from panic, for instance, while watching a man vio-lently flailing his arms at his wife in the passenger seat, huff-ing adrenalin as I approached the car to learn that, in fact, he was a turtlenecked CBC listener, air conducting.

From the corner of his eye, the boy notices me staring protectively, if impotently, and takes enough time to spit ex-pletive threats my way for the girl — she can't be more than fourteen — to move off down the sidewalk at a trot. He throws his cigarette in my direction, before it's taken up into the wind and lands harmlessly in the street.

Pushing up towards the SkyTrain station I made my way

across the street — the violent swearing dimming behind me — past First Avenue, past the Afro Hair Salons and the Portuguese billiards, past the Post Office towards the Van East Theatre. Ricky, used book vendor — and, he says, existentialist — was setting up outside of the credit union, leaning over to fan detritus from his spot with one of his books, the straps of his unzipped backpack laying a loose claim on his forearm as he stooped to sweep.

Silver-black coils are three days grown out of Ricky's half-white complexion when he smiles to acknowledge my arrival.

"Daniel," he said, setting his bag up on the ground and crouching to fish out his merchandise, laying the books side by side. For months, whenever I made the mistake of buying a book brand new, I would almost inevitably chance upon an only-slightly battered copy at Ricky's feet two or three weeks later — too often, the new copy lay still unread in my room at home. Since then, I had made a point of checking in regularly with Ricky. In my new world of letters and unbroken concentration, my re-literacy, he was a primary supplier.

"What's shaking, Ricky? What have you got today?"

"Um," he said, giving the question real thought, calculating my past purchases and mining his memories of our previous conversations for consumer information. "I can't remember, Daniel — Do you like Ondaatje?"

"I haven't really had as much of a chance to read him as I would have liked. My uncle bought me a copy of *Skin of a Lion* two Christmases ago, but I keep forgetting — "

"This," he said, handing me a copy of *Coming Through Slaughter*, "is one of his earlier pieces."

"Right," I answered. "I heard about this. This is way more, like, experimental, no?"

"Yeah, totally."

"How much you want for it?"

"How about three? I'll give it to you with this Baldwin right here for five."

*The Fire Next Time.*

"I like it."

As I gave him the ripped blue five from my change pocket, stinking of pesto, Ricky suddenly became agitated.

"Oh, I need to show you this fucking thing. You're not going to believe this shit." Randy dipped back down into his bag, pulling out a crumpled copy of the *New York Review of Books*. "They've got an article about Chavez, okay, right? Look at the picture they use."

Ricky passed me the issue, turning it around for me to see, lightly touching his thumb to the photo of Venezuelan president Hugo Chavez sitting next to Saddam Hussein.

"I read the article back and forth, okay? It doesn't have a thing to do with the piece. Hussein's name doesn't come up once," he said, smiling with one corner of his mouth and shaking his head. "Unbelievable." It means more to me than I can possibly explain to be around people like Ricky — intellectual enough to read the NRYB, poor enough to be incensed by the slander against Chavez. My favourite people in the world use bus transfers as bookmarks.

Ricky produced an ancient, gossamer Save-On-Foods bag from the pocket of his old bomber to keep the books from getting wet at work. That night's job was out in Port Moody — a newly *petit bourgeois* condominium suburb, abutting the mountainous sprawl of Coquitlam — power-washing the parkade floor underneath a building devoted to residence and retail. The complex is in the middle of a project called Newport Village, offering "Whistler-style living" replete with sushi, pseudo-Italian (but safely WASPish) delis, barbershops, clothing boutiques, and a gaudy Irish Pub that would seem about as familiar to Bobby Sands as the deli would to a visitor from Rome.

Riding the SkyTrain and then bus out to Port Moody in my rainpants and gumboots, I smiled at the young Latino seated across from me and wearing the same kind of uniform — faded denim, in his case, tucked into high rubbers.

"I'm dishwasher," he said, smiling, pointing at his footwear, and then pointing at mine. He had a thin moustache and the short, incredibly thick hair produced by an historical process that began with the Muslim conquest of Spain, then of the Americas by the Spanish. His stop was five minutes after mine, near to where he'd spend the evening washing dishes used by diners at a bar and grill with an entrance opening out into Coquitlam Centre mall. The restaurant closes long after the other shops, he explained, and so they've got another entrance onto the parking lot. As he spoke, the light grey mist against the windows of the bus anticipated an inevitable downpour, just as it did the sopping blowback that would hit me from the parkade floors as I cleaned until midnight.

Scott, my boss, was waiting outside the entrance to the parking lot, leaning up against his van. That he had already unloaded the heavy and cumbersome power washer was testament, I figured, to his being in a good mood.

"Hi, Scott."

"Danny Boy! You all ready to go?"

"I am I am, Scott. How you doing?"

"I'm going fucking crazy, Dan." I hate being called "Dan," the crudest Anglicization of my name. In fact, it was all I could do, as a child, to even adjust to the English pronunciation of "Daniel" that my teachers and fellow students used as they insisted that my father's method (*Dan-yell*) was for girls. "There's a job going on tonight out in Burnaby, and so once you get going I'm off to help get that one done, and I'll swing by tonight around eleven or so to pick up the washer."

"You think I could scam a ride off you, Scott?"

"I can get you to Hastings and Cassiar. Does that help?"

It doesn't.

When first I got the job — whose availability Scott had posted on Craigslist, and which I had come across while looking to sell my bed's headboard for rent money — I had thought that eight-hour shifts hosing down the floors of parking garages was more intellectual downtime than I could justify. I decided, early on, to make use of a section of the library that I had always dismissed, books on tape (or "audiobooks" as they were rendered there, more sensitively, less snobbishly) in order to build my knowledge of the canon, listening to recordings of the great plays and great novels of the ages as I hosed the stalls. On my first outing I had borrowed Eugene O'Neill's *Emperor Jones* and two Arthur Millers: *The Crucible* and *Death of a Salesman*. The plays lasted only half the length of my first shift. And I knew I was in trouble when the time spent listening to *Death of a Salesman* was the least depressing part of my work day.

In many jobs, redundancy of task breeds familiarity with the nuances of otherwise anonymous details. When I worked in the shipping department of a lighting fixture plant, for instance, I learned all the different methods of packing valuable cargo into non-specific, unspecialized boxes using bits of Styrofoam, folded sheets of cardboard, and tape. By the time I was laid off (the "Asian Flu" that began with the fall of the Thai baht in 1998, led to the cancellation of the Asian contracts that are the lifeblood of any Pacific Rim manufacturing concern), I could tell at a glance what strategies would work perfectly to prevent movement and settlement during transportation. When I spent the summer working twelve-hour shifts at Scott Paper, within days I was able to tell — again, on sight — how high and in what pattern different packages had to be stacked before they were tied with twine and taken away by the large paddles of the little vehicle that moved them.

Washing the floors of parkades is not such a job. There are no details to learn, nor any nuances to make the task worth performing for any reason other than the fourteen dollars paid out for each hour that you do it. Cab drivers, say, or really anyone in the service industry, will tell you that looking after so many people every day, one discovers the rich diversity of once-faceless masses. Not so with tending parkade floors. You might think that every oil stain or wad of discarded gum ground into a molecular bond with the pavement through the pressures of time and the wheels of SUVs would bear its own unique imprint, each an urban snowflake in a postmodern, post-climate change winterscape, say.

*No.*

Each stain is virtually the same, and these fall into a few distinct categories: the aforementioned gum; spattered, black or brown, once-fluid stains; generalized brown-or-greyness, made up of filth disseminated enough so as to be noticeable only when it has been partly cleaned, distinguishable only next to an as-yet unwashed patch.

The job requires strength, yes, and with time come the skills that make the performance of one's tasks more *effi*cient as well as more *pro*ficient. But there are no interesting insights to be gained from time invested. Just hours lost and money gained.

There's also, it has to be said, a certain animal — I was going to use "proletarian," but in this usage they're synonyms — attraction about the scene, too. The form-fitting T-shirt, wetted by diffused mists and snug against broad shoulders and hard-working muscles tensing as the equipment is manipulated, the upper body tapering down and then out into the large, yellow rainpants tucked into massive boots. The vision is enough to draw the attention and idle conversational skills of myriad middle-class women and gay men who wouldn't dream, otherwise, of having a real conversation with the type of person who pressure-washes the floors of the parking lot wherein they keep their cars for the eight hours a day they spend at their real jobs.

And that, I assume, is what was behind the brief talk I had with the plump and gorgeous, olive-skinned and large-breasted woman unlocking her Corolla, breathily pronouncing her unintentionally existential small talk:

"Why do they get you to wash the parkade? I would never even notice that!"

I smile at her — *against* her, really — ending our conversation with the obliterating white noise of the power washer. Away from her casually humiliating observations and back to the monotony, solitude, and mental disengagement of my stupid, *stupid*, painful and destructive job.

Destructive because time alone, cordoned off from the sounds of the world by the whirring motor of the machine and the earplugs I'm supposed to wear against the hiss of the stream and the melancholy of Arthur Miller, the mind goes wild on its own. The doctors who study OCD write about something called "Thought-action fusion." A few years ago, two doctors named Whittal and Chodkiewicz wrote a report called "The Paradox of Thought Control in OCD," and in a section called "Cognitive Concepts in OCD," under the heading "Overimportance of Thoughts," they identify the mistaken belief that "having the thought and engaging in the action are the same morally." And in the white noise and enforced meditation of parkade power washing proper perspective — the distinction between thought and reality — disappears along with the three categories of stain.

In fairness, I suppose I did work at least one shift that stood out from the others. Last fall, I was assigned a parkade out in West Point Grey, at a two-level grocery-and-video-store complex near the university, where on the same day as my shift, a colloquium was being held on the subject of a contemporary Robin Hood figure who had become something of a folk hero on the East Side: the Typhoid Mary Blogger.

The Blogger worked for a valet-parking service in and around downtown Vancouver and West Van. Most people had figured that he was an employee of either Starshine Valets or Stanley Parks, but the ambiguity here fueled the legend further. The theory had even been advanced that there were, in fact, several Typhoid Mary Bloggers, doing what they did all over the city at Dundarave, in Yaletown, and posting sometimes-factual, sometimes-fictional accounts of their exploits to the website *typhoidmary.blogspaces.net*.

The *typhoid* blog was a fairly stark, cryptic enterprise, made up merely of lists of extravagant makes of cars. It offered no comment function, no graphics, only a daily-updated list of expensive vehicles, and a haiku, in a cursive font, left justified at the top of the page:

> *Tonight, I was your*
> *valet. Enjoy your meal, friend?*
> *I shit in your car.*

For a few months, the blogger's escapades lit up local news outlets and piqued the civic imagination — fearful, resentful West; bemused, smirking East — prompting, even, a one-act play based on the legend, titled *Stool Pidgin*. Then, as with most things, about a year after the Typhoid Mary Blogger story had lost the interest of the general public, it turned up in academia. It seemed that once it lost its cultural urgency, the story of a young man shitting in the trunks of the wealthy diners whose cars he parked became a vital component of the city's intellectual discourse — a relevance borne out almost by virtue of the broader, coarser society having turned its attention away. The night of the Point Grey job, a long-since tenured political science professor named Marcus Lear was presenting a paper provocatively titled, "From Bin Ladenism to the Typhoid Mary Blogger: the Anarcho-Terrorist Roots of the Baku(ninist)

Tendency of Fatalist Sabotage." The brackets around "nin," it was later explained by the author, were meant as a "rather insouciant punning — marrying the nineteenth century nihilist and pioneer of modern terror, Mikhail Bakunin, with the site of the infamous Soviet Baku Congress, where twentieth century totalitarianism was first wed to Islamist phraseology." My friend Derryl, whose UBC log-in sponsored my library research, was a student of Lear's at the time and had forwarded me information on the talk. Making my way to the Endowment Lands early, I sat my rainpants down behind rows of tweed, three hours before my shift.

There were thirty or forty people gathered in the small auditorium where Lear was to speak. Mostly grad students and younger faculty sat well-dressed and eager towards the front of the audience, while greying, professorial types filed in slowly towards the back. To the side of the auditorium, a wide-hipped woman with cropped brown hair showed off an infant, which she held in her arms. I winced against the images in mind of hurting the child — fast-moving pictures in my mind's eye that I knew would distract me from the symposium. Lear sat onstage, behind a table, fixing a microphone to his lapel. A young man wearing a bow tie and parted hair introduced him sycophantically, and Lear rose to a polite applause in anticipation of his remarks, moving elegantly behind the podium, and I exhaled in relief as the young mother left the room with her baby, freeing me somewhat from my OCD obligations.

"A great many thinkers from across the political spectrum — and I pause to add, here, for any of those who might seek to identify an essential conservatism in the thesis that I'll advance today, Harper's Lewis Lapham is among them —

have lucidly delineated the shared discursive space inhabited by, on the one hand, the bin Ladenist terrorists of al-Qaeda and, I would argue by extension, the suicide mission-runners of the Palestinian and Iraqi insurgencies and, on the other hand, the nineteenth-century European traditions of anarchism and narodnism; the proponents of propaganda by the deed, as it were." The professor paused to take a long sip from the bottled water set on the table. He arched his grey eyebrows up over his rimless eyeglasses as he glanced sidelong at his notes. "We can therefore take, as a starting point, the existence of a galvanizing and violent commonality in the shared philosophical realm of those who purport to carry out the religio-historical tasks of the Muslim world as well as those of the underclasses of the West. But here I'm going to emphasize the shared space of sabotage that employs the *body* as a weapon, and I'm going to place particular emphasis on the body as a purveyor of *disease* and *sickness*, and I'm talking both about the body as well as, in the case of al-Qaeda, the sickness and toxicity of the body politic. Because, like the original Typhoid Mary, who either wilfully or negligently infected her social superiors and was therefore retrieved by the scatalogically obsessed Blogger in a misdirected bit of populism, al-Qaeda thrust themselves forward as spokespersons for a pathological supranational body that, like Typhoid Mary, seeks to bring us down with her. And I hope that none of you will be too displeased by my so closely pairing the scatological with the eschatological." Light, polite laughter here — except from Bow Tie, who'd never in his life heard a more brilliant joke, and sat braying in the front row for far too long.

Lear went on like that for a little over an hour. Halfway

through, my hands were shaking with rage, but by the end of the speech my legs were asleep and my neck hurt. As the assembled crowd applauded the talk, and Lear made his way to back to his seat, I jumped from mine in favour of a spot leaning against the wall, where — with a better view of the crowd — I looked for hope in the potential of rebuttal. I wasn't going to offer one, dressed as I was.

As a rule, in my experience, conservative academics wear large gold rings. Progressive academics wear large silver earrings. I was emboldened, then, when a tawny woman in her early forties, very clearly a faculty member from the confidence with which she carried herself, raised her left hand to speak (sending a thick, wooden bracelet up the length of her upturned forearm) while fixing her short brown hair behind massive silver earrings with her right.

"Dr. Lear," she started, in a dry and unbending voice. "I want to thank you for your remarks today. I would, however, like to address what I see as a fundamental analytical component missing from your essay." This is it, I thought hopefully — the cavalry rides in from the left. "I think we need to talk about the element of transgressive gender play here, where a young man, or young men, assume the identity of a racialized-Irish *female* domestic..."

As the older faculty in the back rows began to giggle and scoff, I pushed up the stairs and out the exit door quietly, alone and still far too early for my shift.

That night I threw the gun down onto the floor of the lot, turning off the machine to prevent the pressure from building up. In solidarity with the Typhoid Mary Blogger, I took my prick in my hands and pissed all over the corner stall, staining the cloudy brown water that I'd left with a spreading yellow. Smiling, muttering obscenities, stealing glances over my shoulder, I thought about rich Point Grey fucks parking there, walking in my piss and, in the best case scenario, dropping their groceries in it as they loaded cars that cost more than I'll ever make to drive home to houses I'll never see the insides of. I thought about my sweet, pissy revenge on the ruling class of Vancouver as I restarted the machine and erased what I'd done.

# V

"So it's just: 'Splitz has the great taste of vanilla and banana, with none of the calories'? That's all you need for now?"

"The rest of it recorded perfect last time," said the tech, scratching the patchy growth underneath his chin and jaw with knuckles of a more consistent hairiness. "So yeah, let's do five or six, vault 'em, and then that's done and you and I can both get out of here. Get home for Thanksgiving."

"Actually, I'm just sticking around LA. There's no holiday back home, Canadian Thanksgiving is in October. So I'm just going to hang around LA."

Ty had spent the last three days in the recording studio for a two-day job, watching technicians prepare and directors going over scripts with company representatives. He couldn't help but suspect that Al Sampson wouldn't have been made to wait through all of it. They would have sent someone to wait for Sampson, to page him when it was time to record. But Ty had to wait.

As time passed — Sampson's body was re-learning muscle control, simple and complex movements, the bending of joints — Ty's American management met with Sampson's to discuss extending the breadth of the substitution. It was stressed, from Ty's end, that there was no reason the soundalike couldn't follow through on Sampson's myriad, continuing endorsement deals, radio and television voiceover work for advertisers. It was win-win-win: advertisers got an aural likeness for a drastic cut in price, a commission went to Sampson, and Ty made some extra coin.

"Into the mic whenever you're ready."

"Splitz has the great taste of vanilla *and* banana, with none of the calories."

"Again."

"Splitz has the great *taste* of vanilla and banana, with none of the calories."

"Ty, don't emphasize 'taste' like that," chimed a thin-faced writer-director who stood effetely behind the technician, leaning over to press the button that channelled his voice into the booth. "It makes it sound artificial." The tech laughed.

"Again."

"Splitz has the great taste of *vanilla* and *banana*, with none of the calories."

"Again."

"Splitz has the *great* taste of vanilla *and* banana, with *none* of the calories."

"Good."

"Again."

"Splitz has the — sorry."

"Again."

"Splitz has the fantastic taste of — sorry. I guess that's not — do you need me to say great?"

"It's a time thing, Tyler. Just stick to the script."

"Sure."

"Again when you're ready."

"Splitz has the great taste of vanilla and banana, with *none of the calories.*"

"And one final one."

"Splitz has the great taste of vanilla and banana, *with* none of the calories."

"I'm good," said the technician, flipping switches and pulling his headphones off his ears, turning them in one hand so as to wind the cord around the set.

"Thanks guys," said the director in the sweep of the same gently contemptuous motion with which he moved to the door.

Ty removed his own headphones, trying a few times, unsuccessfully, to hang them around the microphone in front of him. Finally, he balanced them on the black vinyl stool that stood next to him.

"Hey," said the tech, leaning over the microphone that allowed him to communicate with Ty through the sound-proofing. "When's Al Sampson coming back? We miss that guy."

"I don't know, man. I'm not his — I wouldn't know."

"Tell that guy we miss him. A very talented man."

"I would have thought it's better for you guys while he's sick. I'm getting like less than a third of what he gets for recording these things. Even with the money that's still going to him, it's so much cheaper to use me."

"I'm union, guy. That's got nothing to do with me; I get the same thing for working the panel whatever — whoever's in the booth. But Al Sampson always makes me laugh."

*Fucking asshole.*

In the car, Ty thought again about how odd it is to grow up in Vancouver thinking of Los Angeles as such a big, important city. The myth stood in such heavy contrast to the low sprawl of the living city. And the blacks — he has had to admit, though only to other white people, and with all the necessary cushioning of sensitivity — it's very different being in a city where there are blacks. As he had told the comedians back in Vancouver in a late-night posting to the message-board used by the city's comics, it was as though someone had exchanged all of the Asians he was familiar with for Africans; and what at home would have been done by Sikhs — farm labour, house-building — is here done by Mexicans. He could easily do the Corner Store Character down here.

The traffic on the way to the studio was slow moving, an unglamorous captivity of combustive energies and carcinogens, crawling and angry. Ty pulled on an iced coffee — he still couldn't believe that the Americans didn't sweeten their iced tea — moving it over towards the cup-holder, a third too small to cradle the drink.

"Fuck," he said, the satellite radio playing unobtrusive electronic music by a New York group called Solipseismic. "Super size me," laughed Ty, noticing a fingerprint on his sunglasses. "Shit." He took the sunglasses — large, aviator, expensive — from his face and spat into the corner that was smudged. Squeezing his drink between his chilling knees, he circled the lens with the edge of his grey T-shirt.

Ty showed his pass to the parking lot attendant, and pulled into the space reserved for him next to the Army Brats building, wondering again why it was that he shouldn't get Sampson's parking space while he was off the show. He closed the car door with his hip, pulling the plastic dome off of his cup and swallowing the rest of his coffee, spitting the ice cubes onto the concrete after they'd been cleaned of cream and sugar.

On the way to the reading room, where the cast and writers would meet to discuss the edits to the scripts they'd seen on Monday, Ty turned into the kitchen to grab one of the bottles of San Pellegrino that he'd stored inside the door of the communal fridge. He'd thrown away the thin, waxed box in which the bottles came in groups of four, and marked his name in sharpie ink on the individual labels of each.

As he entered the room, he immediately noticed Debbie Hunting, leaning over the sink, her embroidered black silk pants pulling tight; pulling the corners of his mouth; pulling the fly of his jeans.

For a few seconds, he stared and smiled, quietly, before realizing that Debbie's shoulders were shaking. Turning to leave the room, Ty squeaked his heel against the tiled floor and Debbie spun, quickly, her face red and swollen.

"Hey," she said.

"Hi, Debbie. Do you want me to — Are you okay?"

"Yeah, I'll be fine, Tyler." She paused, and Ty made his way slowly towards the fridge. "I just miss Al, that's all."

"Oh."

"Yeah." Debbie delivered the last as an adult speaks of tragedy to child, without the expectation of understanding.

"He was — you guys were pretty close, huh?"

"We are, yeah." Debbie's auburn hair hung straight and thick against her jaw, the hair on her forehead matted with a quiet sweating. She produced a dried and crumpled Kleenex from her sleeve, like an old woman, wiping her nose and then dabbing her eyes.

"Were you guys ever — I don't know."

"What?"

"You know. I mean," he drew his breath for courage. "You *know* you're really pretty, Debbie."

Debbie was already staring at the ceiling, drying the corner of one of her eyes, and so she had no need to roll them when she let out an exasperated sound, the sort of sighing grunt expelling air and respect: the hasty return from generosity to the familiarity of an accurate first impression.

"No, Tyler. Never mind."

"Sorry."

"It's fine."

"I just think you're very –"

"It's fine, Tyler, thank you."

He snapped the seal on the mineral water, cracking the cap like knuckles.

"I hope they fixed up that supermarket scene, hey? That thing was just way too long. Hardly any payoff."

"I hope they fixed it too."

"Hey you guys," piped Sammy Mallick, standing at the doorway.

"Hey Sam."

"Oh, Sammy," said Debbie, throwing her arms around Sammy's neck. Sammy laughing softly onto her shoulder, stroking the back of her hair. Ty stood back, sipping the mineral water.

"I know, sweetie, I know. It's tough, baby, isn't it? But you gotta pull together, Debbie. You know?"

Debbie pulled back, nodding, gulping air. "Yeah."

"Why don't you run and wash up in the restroom, sweetheart? I'll put on the kettle for you, make you some tea."

"Thanks Sammy," she said, kissing him on the cheek before briskly leaving the room. Sammy took the white electric kettle from beside the fridge over to the sink, emptying the stale water and filling it afresh. He went over to a cupboard filled haphazardly with teabags long since unattached to any labeled boxes, and so began to pick through them by scent, holding them near to his long, impressive nose with its massive, fatherly nostrils.

"She's having a tough time with this Al stuff lately," he said to Ty.

"But it sounds like he's doing pretty good."

"All things considered lately, it seems so, yeah."

"You guys are pretty close, hey?"

"Who, me and Deb?"

"Yeah."

"Sure. We go to church together."

"Really?"

"Yeah."

Ty frowned, spinning his water in the bottle, while Sammy settled on a tea.

"I thought you were Palestinian, Sammy."

"I am."

"But wouldn't that — aren't you Muslim?"

"No, I'm Greek Orthodox, same as Debbie. Lots of Orthodox Christians in Palestine."

"Hunh. I didn't know that."

"Most people don't," Sammy sang.

"Wow, I totally didn't know that."

"Yes," said Sammy, very slightly losing patience. "We even have a couple of biblical sites in Palestine, you know, like, small-time stuff. Pretty marginal to Christianity, like Bethlehem, Jerusalem." Sammy smiled.

"Is that true?"

"Jesus, man, I thought Americans were supposed to be the dummies when it comes to geography. They don't teach you this stuff in Canada?"

"No — at least, I don't think so."

"Hm."

"Watched pot never boils."

"Pardon?"

"Watched pot never boils," Ty smiled. "You're staring at the thing."

"Yeah, I put too much water in, I think."

Ty sat down at the table in the centre of the room, drawing his toe along the tiles, leaving a small mark.

"I don't think Debbie likes me at all, Sam."

"What makes you say that?"

"I don't know."

Sammy kept leaning daintily, palms down and wrists in, staring at the kettle, avoiding eye contact with Ty. He felt Ty's empty eyes on his back, though, boring, and boring, and so finally, turning up to look at the cupboards: "Debbie misses Al, Ty. I mean, we all do. She's, you know — "

Ty dropped his eyes, staring at the green bottle in his hands, picking at the label with his thumbs. "Yeah, I know," he said, starting to.

# VI

The single-mug filter drip is, I would argue, the most depressing method devised for the preparation of coffee. In the homes of big families, or even couples, a real, true-to-life coffee machine — implying the presence of the *social* by brewing drinks for more than one — serves, at least, to remind the consumer why it is that he or she is up early enough to need coffee in the first place: *A rewarding life with the person or persons with whom I'm sharing this pot makes drugging myself into alertness not only reasonable, but comforting. Have you seen the paper this morning?*

Standing in the kitchen of my suite pouring, in instalments, the boiled contents of an electric kettle into a small brown funnel that balances atop my mug provides no such reassurance, particularly since I used the same kettle to prepare the NeoCitran with which I medicated myself into sleep the night before.

Mug in hand, ignoring the small spills onto the peeling vinyl floor of the kitchen, I made my way over to the computer, waking the sleeping machine by shaking the mouse on its pad and sitting on the broken swivel chair picked up from a socially mobile former roommate in a past move. As the screen came to life, my eyes widened. I had forgotten to shut the web browser with which I had been trolling pornography into the small hours of the morning before going to bed. It's too early now for what last night seemed so enticing, and so *LatinaBoulevard.com* is traded hastily for Hotmail.

Nearly a month ago, Gary had made his way downstairs, tapping on the window, to announce grimly that they would need him again in Halifax for the once-hypothetical transfusion. The last chance his brother had against a full and revitalized return of the illness was the replacement of his bone marrow. I'd shaken my head grimly, fighting back the memories of my mother's operation, biting back my own story, with its nightmare ending, hoping to save Gary from the pessimism he had the rest of his life to host. Here he was in my inbox again, subject line "Update."

Dear Daniel,

Decided to take a few minutes and let you know that I'll be home in another two weeks. We'll figure something out about your rent. I'm not too worried. Truth to tell, I'm happy to write it off as homecare and house-sitting for the month. That way you can go ahead and make some Visa payments or something. Do you have a Visa card?

The procedure happened two days ago, and from any of the indicators they use this early into things, it went very well. They knocked me out completely and I reacted very poorly to the general anaesthetic. Every goddamn time I sneeze the last few days I grab my hips because something inside me says they'll shatter without my support. Like a boxer with a glass eye. Travis seems to be responding well. Rosa has been mothering the two of us, looking after grown men as though we were children, which has been weird for her since it runs against forty-five years of feminist upbringing.

The whole thing has been a trip, Daniel, and I mean it. The past few weeks have thrown the past thirty years of my life into such sharp and unkind focus that I wanted to reach out. This email's got more to do with that, in the end, than it does with rent relief or travel schedules.

Rosa's been giving me peppermint tea for my stomach, the herbal shit, the sort of petty bourgeois junk I would have thrown against the wall a month ago. It tastes okay, and it helps my stomach.

Gary

○

"What do you call an *apna* porn star?"

"I call him Bo."

"No, fuck off. Seriously, what do you call a Punjabi porn star?"

"What?"

"Balls Deep."

Without any regular, friendly contact with white racists

in my life, Baljinder — Bo — had quickly become my lone source for comedic prejudice, at least as directed against South Asians. Smiling from behind his beard and underneath the doo-rag skully he wore today in place of a turban, Bo rolled the weed I'd given him atop an issue of *The New Yorker* and giggled off the resin of his pun.

There are two things I have never done which — given that I was born and raised in and around Vancouver — are nearly impossible and wholly incredible. The first is that I have never, in my life, skied, which is akin in this city to discovering as an adult that, in fact, the language you speak is an only-sometimes comprehensible dialect of everyone else's. For a region whose every economic seduction — by Hollywood or real estate, Expo or the Olympics — has climbed and fallen at inclines sharp enough to split the hairs shed by $1500 designer dogs, the act of summiting mountains in order to barrel down them has become a collective catharsis that gives the whole thing the illusion of forethought.

The second is that I have never rolled a joint. But rolling marijuana is, to me, like buying it — why would you do it yourself when you know that at some point it will be taken care of? Bo, not much of a skier either, was set to work on rolling, coughing loudly as he did so and upsetting the weed, blowing small leaves out of the Zig-Zag and down onto its perch, an American magazine full of essays by writers who most definitely had the time, money, and inclination to make room for ski trips.

There was a time when I used to agonize over the stupidity of my pot indulgence, given the havoc it wrought on my thinking. I achieved some insight into the paradox from an unlikely source of inspiration when an old, lactose-intolerant friend from high school had excused himself from a poker game to shit for an hour and half, before returning to the table for another slice of the pizza that had sent him there. I guess I believe that there's a perfect high for me somewhere, if I can keep myself from smoking too much or not enough, if I can avoid harsh pesticides or visions of hydroponic-induced growth in a basement or crawl space. Bo has a line to some Gulf Island lousy with hippies, where the drugs are grown with wind and sunshine. I'm hopeful.

Neither Bo nor I is sure whether he gets stares because he is a *sardar* — a beard- and turban-wearing Sikh — or because he stands 6'4" (before turban) and the needle on his scale pushes past three-hundred like a truck passing highway weigh-ins. Likely, we think, it's a combination of both. Regardless, and despite feeling immense guilt for sympathizing with such an unsavoury character, I can't help but feel sorry for the unfortunate white kid who cut off a clump of Bo's hair in elementary school, sneering, "Now you won't get into Heaven" before being beaten with the kind of severity normally on hold until at least junior high.

Baljinder and I met at Langara, while he was working on the student paper, *The Gleaner*, and sleeping with as many white girls as he could before his father — a religious figure of some prominence in the smallish, sectarian offshoot of Sikhism practised by his family — put his foot down and insisted on marriage to a nice, *Jatt*, Sikh. (Bo's passionate and technically accurate tirades about Sikhism's early rejection of caste were launched against his shrugging father to no avail.) The parental edict had, in a sense, backfired, since the pressures of a looming, endogamous betrothal ensured that Bo wouldn't bother giving the time of day to Punjabi girls so long as he was single.

His parents didn't have to convince him, though, of the superiority of all Indian dishes.

The exterior of Main Street's Sind Sweets is a tacky gallery of reds and yellows, with loud pennants of fading colour announcing the celebrations of Sikh holidays long since passed. Inside, a banner reading "Happy Birthday" is strung permanently against the back wall, and sullen staff come in and out of the kitchen without smiling, bringing plates still crackling with heat to Indian customers who know well enough to order à la carte, while white patrons line the buffet, filling plates with foods they want to wrap their tongues around first verbally, then literally. Half a block up the street is the more popular Flavours of India Buffet, always packed with whites, East Asians, and other non-Indian diners. Those who really know Little India, though, made their way south — twenty steps past Punjabi Insurance and ten past the women fingering the myriad fabrics at Nurmal's — to eat at Sind. À la carte.

Baljinder had been eating à la carte since childhood, when his mother would enlist his aid in carrying bags of flours and spices from a neighbouring shop by promising him lunch at Sind Sweets afterwards. More than twenty years after his first visit, he and I found ourselves deep in conversation in the offices of the *Gleaner*, impressed with each other's sarcasm. I walked with him over to Sind for a tutorial in avoiding the buffet — a session which instilled in me a self-loathing contempt for the queue of *goray* greedily heaping hours-old *daal* and chicken into the indented sections of their tin plates. Resplendent with dignity, we sat and waited for menus. Within forty minutes of sitting down, and just two or three hours after meeting each other, Bo and I found ourselves in a comfortable back and forth. That's why, when I advanced my own theories about Indian cuisine, Bo laughed, sparring in good humour:

"My feeling really is that — in the world, people, countries, they're either entrée people, or they're sweets and desserts people. It seems to me — like it's an inverse relationship where the worse your real food is, the more emphasis you place on sweets as a country. Look at England. Look how much candy and shit they've got? The Scottish with the deep-fried Mars bars, the Germans with their chocolate. So if I say you guys have terrible desserts, you should be thrilled. Nobody's got main courses locked down like you guys. Or appetizers. But the desserts are shit, Bo. If multiculturalism is going to work in this country, you know — I mean look, I'm sure that I hate white people just as much as you do, and on balance, sure, we could lose Europe, no question. But desserts are the one thing the continent did right."

Bo smiled, raising an eyebrow: "What about *gulab jamun?*"

"*Gulab jamun* is the exception that proves the rule," I shot back with affected anger. "Listening to brown people talk about *gulab jamun* is like listening to white people talk about the Beatles or Steve Nash. It's pathetic. Get over it, man. *Gulab jamun* is Benny Goodman; it's an aberration. In a cosmic sense, it never even happened. It's Dave Brubeck."

"Well, then the Chinese too," he said, deflecting, which I took for victory.

"Hey, you get no arguments from me," I offered magnanimously.

"Fucking red bean? In a dessert?"

"I know, man, I know," I'd said, covering my broad smile, projecting this new friendship into the future like a crush.

"People always say 'Oh, the Chinese are so thin, it's a mystery,'" he said, curling his face up in pretended contempt. "Try the desserts. Mystery fucking solved."

I laughed out loud, him too, as curious, bearded faces turned towards our table.

"So what, do you guys have good desserts?" he asked finally.

"What do you think? Outside Montréal, besides mining asbestos and humping each other, people in Québec have been doing nothing but tapping maple trees for four hundred years."

"A rising sap people all around."

"That's right, *mon ami. C'est vrai.* Hah, rising sap peepull."

"Did your dad ever do that stuff for you guys? The boiled maple syrup on the snow? At my elementary school, when they taught us about *Carnivale* or whatever, they taught us about that thing. I forget if it has a name."

"Yeah, a *tire.* The one or two nights a year it snows enough in Vancouver to do one, yeah, my dad did it for us. It's good stuff, man." I noted to myself that the next time I visited him, during the winter, I ought to get him to do it again. "The tins with the snowscape on them, with the syrup clear as apple juice, running just as fast. My grandfather used to send them out. Those cans were Québec to me and my little brother."

"When did he come out here, your dad?"

"Nineteen seventy-five, I think. It was one of Trudeau's first cultural exchanges between French and English Canada — send the army in and, over the ensuing years, the hippies trickle out."

"My parents came out the same time. Nineteen seventy-four."

"Pierre's two very different faces."

"And here we are."

"My dad was part of a whole generation of frogs that came out here for weed, warm weather, and then after French Immersion, became an army of teachers. I mean just all of them, whatever they were doing, one buddy of my dad's was a butcher, they all became teachers. Training English kids for a bilingual country that never happened. Nothing like that will ever happen again. *Papa* moved back to Ste. Thérèse a while ago now. I talk to him every week or two, and his English is already starting to rust."

"What about your little brother?"

"He's living in Montréal, and it's made him more English than ever."

After dinner, we'd walked out onto Main Street — already closing down for the evening. Like all ethnic satellites for now-suburban communities, the sun set here into loneliness — and Bo offered me a ride.

"You want a lift, Daniel? I'm headed home"

"Where's home, Bo?"

"New West."

"Could you take Highway One? Gimme a lift down near Commercial and First?"

"Fuck it, I'll drive you home," he'd said, waving his keys, dismissing the hassle.

"You sure?"

"Why not."

"Thanks, man."

"No worries. I feel bad about your Little India experience, it's the least I could do."

"Why should you feel bad?"

"Oh," he had said, lifting his moustache with the ends of his mouth, pushing his face into a wide-smiling remembrance, "this place used to be so much more lively. Even the alleyways, when I was a kid. Like something out of *Godfather Two*, but for us. These days, the weight has shifted to Surrey."

"You know, I was born at Surrey Memorial, spent my first few years out there," I said, for the sake of authenticity.

"A Surrey *gora*, imagine that. Who'd thought we could get along so well?" He broke away from the sidewalk, crossing the front bumper of his car to the driver's door. "I'll take you out there some day if you want, show you the insider track. The secret handshake shit."

"Then I'll take you to Maillardville," I offered back.

"Maillardville."

"Maillardville," I'd answered, drawing the name out and smiling. "But of course. First Québecois settlement in British Columbia."

"Yeah, they taught us *that*," Bo shot back, his emphasis confusing me. He took the keys out of his pocket and we got into his car, a gold Toyota, which prompted him to joke: "You'd think we'd have learned our lesson about traveling the West Coast in Japanese vessels."

As we drove down Main, the silence in the car was

heavy. Finally, Bo had spoken again:

"You want to know something else about Maillardville?"

"Sure."

"First settlement of French-Canadians out here, right? But you know how they got here? Or, I guess, you know why they were brought here?"

"Why?"

"The mill out there used to employ tons of Sikh labourers. It was a huge employer of Punjabis, at, you know, very low wages or whatever. And you know how the labour movement and everybody was totally anti-Punjabi, the whole Komagata Maru-type crowd? Asian exclusion and everything? And anyway, they pressured the company to hire white workers. And so they fired the Punjabis, and they brought in the Québecois. And that's how Maillardville started."

"Jesus," I'd said. And then repeated it: "*Jesus*."

"Hey," he said, turning briefly from the road to look at me. "I don't know why I said that. That was hostile. There was — anyways, just forget I said it, okay?"

"No, of course."

We sat in silence down the length of Main Street, past the twenties and the teen avenues, where the hipsters had colonized huge swathes of what had once been East Vancouver. Further down, we passed the Ukrainian church, the Bike Co-Op and St. Patrick's — the congregation of which filled the cafeteria-style Filipino restaurants across the street every Sunday afternoon. The bingo hall came and went on the left as we crossed Broadway, pushing past light industry, garages, and motels. As we approached Main and Terminal, set to turn right, a squeegee kid approached the car not waiting for Bo's nod to go ahead and wash the windows.

"Bet you that's one of mine."

"Bet you're right." When the kid made his way around to the driver's side to collect his loonie, I leaned across Bo's lap.

"*Es-tu Québecois?*"

"*Ouais*," he answered, jerking his head to move the limp punkrock hairdo that hung in his eyes. Between the Oka Standoff and Vancouver squeegees, I thought, we are a people known almost exclusively, in Western Canada, as those who either oppress or grow Mohawks.

"*Ça fait combien de temps que t'es ici?*"

"*J'viens tout-juste d'arriver. J'travaillais dans les champs de l'Okanagan.*"

I'd smiled. "*Travaillais-tu avec beaucoup d'gens comme lui?*" I jerked a thumb towards Bo, and the squeegee kid smiled.

"*Ouais.*"

"*Salut*, bye, *mon homme. Prend soins de toi. Fait attention.*"

Bo gassed the car and turned onto Terminal.

"What did he say?"

I sighed.

"He said the squeegee kid at that intersection used to be Sikh, but he was brought in to replace him."

Baljinder shook his head, smiling. "That's bad, yo."

"He said he's just got in from the Okanagan, picking fruit. I asked him if he was working with a lot of people who looked like you, and he said he was."

"There you go, buddy. Don't feel too guilty about Maillardville. We'll always have the orchards. I mean, they hanged your guy to drive home a point."

"De Lorimier?"

"Sure. I meant Louis Riel, I think, but there you go. They hanged those guys, they hanged Bhagat Singh, and now they've got us all huffing pesticides and picking fruits for the Commonwealth." He smiled wryly. "You'd don't have a thing to feel guilty about, *gora*."

"You know when my Dad was a kid, growing up in Ste. Rose, you know the name of the place they went for their summer vacations?"

"What's that?"

"Old Orchard." I rested for punctuation. "You like that?"

"No," Bo said, still smiling. "I don't think that's funny at all."

Even in childhood, with its fast and arbitrary social coupling and uncoupling, I'd never cemented a friendship this quickly. Over movies, books, and women we rolled with laughter, debated, commiserated. Three years later, Baljinder was at my house for several visits a week, this time sitting on the couch and rolling a preparatory joint on top of my magazine, readying our dime bag for consumption as we headed out the door for what was meant to be a show in the sky.

"You know, I googled this thing –"

"What did you google? What terms?" he interjected impatiently.

"I don't know — I googled 'meteor shower vancouver.' Anyways, the point is, nothing came up about tonight at all."

"Fuck that. A general Google search on meteor shower –"

"No, I did a news search."

"Fuck man, I don't know — whatever."

"Who is this guy?"

"I don't know man, some *desi*. Some," he smiled, "FOB at temple who seemed very knowledgeable about astronomy, and he said tonight the sky is going to light up. He said that there's some big meteor shower happening that will peak from fucking — what was it? Like midnight."

"Did he give you, like, a name or anything? Is there — is there like a name for the, whatever, *phenomenon*? We could look that up."

"*Ma da choud*, Dan-yell," he said, looking up at me with exasperation and dropping his work with frustration. "At the very, very worst, what happens? We have a nice spring drive out to Chilliwack, we smoke what will be, if you let me concentrate, one of the great joints of my career, and we watch a beautiful sky that would, on the most uneventful night of the year, look like a laser show to your light-pollution addled eyes. That is, as far as I can tell, the worst-case scenario. In the best case, doctor Golden Temple's promise makes good, and we watch a show."

On the advice of Bo's anonymous *gurdwara* source, we were headed out to the same lake outside of Chilliwack where, for the past several years, we'd watched the Perseid meteor shower every summer, high as kites and uttering the kind of pretentious silliness that stoned observers of the cosmos have eternally passed off as meditation on the smallness of enormity and the enormity of smallness; the kind of shit that stands in for philosophy in a province where marijuana sales are measured in the billions (if we're going to be properly materialist about it).

As we drove towards the suburbs, I thought of *Turtle-*

*doves* and of Nicole, and when we passed one of the Surrey exits, in the car that Bo had borrowed from his brother, I absent-mindedly slipped into stupid, stunted whiteness:

"Bo, do you know a lady named Gurmit Sihota, out in Surrey?"

Bo grimaced. He expected more from me than the stock *gora* assumption that all Indians know each other, and let me know, in no uncertain terms. He bobbed his head as though it were top-heavy, sticking an index finger into the air, mock-coolie.

"Oh yes, she is my seventh cousin," he said, looking out through the windshield. "We shall be married at the request of my family, thank you!"

"No, Bo," I started, embarrassed, trying to apologize.

"Who is Gurmit Sihota?"

"She's this lady with the NDP out in Surrey, I don't know. Apparently she has been a real help to Nicole in this whole book-banning thing."

"Right. Hey tell me, this guy out there, what is his name?"

"The Pastor? The fascist?"

"Yeah."

"Gerry."

"Does he have, like, a really skinny son?"

"I have no idea."

"What's his name again?"

"Gerry."

"*That's* right. This guy is going out of his way to court *apnay* on this issue. Not just Sikhs, either. Muslims. I think he is trying to get some of the Chinese and Arab groups out there to sign on, turn the whole homophobic freak show into some kind of multicultural — "

"I know, it's –"

"No, let me tell you what it is. Like, whatever, ten or twelve years ago my cousin was hurt badly in one of these lunch-hour race wars that used to be so bad out in Surrey. They found out years later, by the way, that one of the white guys who did it was into some weird shit, these sort of loose neo-Nazi affiliations."

"Jesus."

"Anyhow, at the time, white kids and brown kids were both getting seriously fucked up, there was a *gora* kid got put in a wheelchair, shit like that. And this fucker Gerry, he was all over the news as the white hero. He was talking in broad terms, you know, youth violence and shit, but the point of his take was pretty — you know the loose metaphors they speak in? Our *community*, they say, or they talk about how bad things are *getting*, or about how this *used* to be a lovely place to live. And now what? Less than a decade later, and these fuckers from the temple are lining up to stand next to him at press conferences to keep white faggots away from their kids. It blows my mind."

We sat quietly for a few minutes as the mix CD that Bo had burned passed from Charlie Mingus's "Fables of Faubus" to John Coltrane's "India." The sharply beautiful whine of the soprano saxophone and the liquidity of the crash symbols played by Elvin Jones worked against the backdrop of the hulking green and blue mountains cradling our drive. We passed the Dino-Town theme park that had risen from the ashes of the old Flintstones' Village where, as children, we'd driven pedal-operated versions of Fred and Barney's car, or paddled canoes with Cretaceous wordplay painted in thick, cartoonish black letters on their sides.

I thought of Nicole's hair falling out onto her pillow, into the drain of the shower she shared with my cousin, or else pulled out by the tines of her thick wooden brush and laid down on the oak vanity in their bedroom. I thought about Gary sitting beside a brother who had become a stranger as the result of obstinate, dogmatic politics divorced from the humanist impetuses that were supposed to have moved them in the first place. Bo's beaten cousin and some white proto-thug with his legs and spine cracked. The echoes of millions of human bodies run through ten times as many batterings and sicknesses pounded on the insides of my head as I tried to keep up with the pace of the injuries, mentally assigning them bandages, radiation, shots, pills, crutches, canes, wheelchairs, ice packs, heat, MRIs, CAT scans, pacemakers, defibrillators, therapies, and euthanasia. I thought about Mom. I imagined two pieces of gauze fixed over my eyes with medical tape, smiling to myself as the harshness melted first into filtered shadows and then into nothing, Coltrane screeching another sublime crescendo as we came closer to the park.

We lay next to each other in the cold, dry sand looking up at a sky that was — regardless of what turned out to be the inaccuracy of the good doctor's prediction of meteoric fireworks — exquisite, clouded with the interstellar tufts of galaxy that web the stars, pubic hairs on heavenly bodies, invisible from the city but pronounced out here in the blue-blackness of unchallenged rural night. Bo sat up for a moment and lit the joint, inhaled deeply and repeatedly and passed it to me as he blew out a cloud of purplish smoke with a piercing cough. I pulled and tasted, concentrating, feeling as though hot blood was filling my lungs and foaming up along their edges. Halfway through my first exhalation I inhaled again, deeper, into my stomach, pulling the smoke into the veins of my arms, along into my fingers and firing out of the sides of my elbows. Even as I passed it back to Bo, I felt the numbness crawling up and around the backs of my ears, expanding across the top of my head like a skullcap, trickling down my forehead and behind my eyes as I coughed the hot smoke out of my lungs. Taking the joint back between my index and thumb I drew again, with my pulse now sounding loudly in my ears and down through the rest of my body.

I got up and walked over into the darkness of the bushes, bracing against stoned panic, and took myself into my hands, pissing so strongly and ecstatically into the leaves that it felt like ejaculate. I smiled broadly and whispered to myself, giggling. After pissing I rolled it around with my fingers, with the shimmering paralysis of my skin sending wild trills of pleasure back into my spine and up to the base of my skull. Very suddenly I was masturbating, drawing short, insufficient staccato breaths in to oxygenize the orgasmic process, thinking of the enormous breasts and olive skin of the middle class lady who had left me invisible and non-existent, without purpose, blowing the gum off the ground where she parked her car. Now she was resting on her knees and the palms of her hands — for a flickering second, the fantasy is interrupted by some terrorizing violent image, full of knives and blood, but I grit my teeth — her thick hair hanging down and damp around her shoulders as she looks back to watch me pound my hips into the enormity of her thighs and ass — once again interrupted, but I move past it.

This is nothing new, although the head of my penis shrinks a little under the unarousing weight of the intrusive thoughts. The sweat is beading on the surface of her brown skin marked only by the fading imprints of my tightening grip as she grows more and more obscene while I approach climax, calling me "Daddy" — then one last interruption — and then moaning, I blow my finish into the bushes and down the back of my knuckles, screaming with stoned pleasure as my whole body convulsed with the strength of the arrival. Bo called out from the beach, and I said I'd be a second. I wiped my knuckles on the sand, made my way to the edge of the water to wash up, then lay back next to Bo, whose body warmth glowed against the chill.

"Dude, man — you remember what you said back at my house about the worst case scenario? I'm going to call you 'Panglosse' now."

Bo let a shotgun laugh out through gritted teeth. "That doesn't make any sense, Daniel."

"Yes it does," I said, giggling now myself. "Because you said 'worst case scenario,' but it was, like, still good. So you're like — It's like the best of all possible worlds."

"Cool, man," said Bo sarcastically. "Hey, remind me to lend you that *Voltaire for Fucking Idiots* book that I — "

The end of his sentence was obscured by my and then his erupting laughter, a fit thereof leading into a wild frenzy of coughing and more laughs.

"This fucking guy," he said. "There's no meteors."

I started a trench in the sand with the heel of my foot, pushing lightly from left to right, trying to keep my mind from wandering. Bo pulled a pack of gum from the pocket of his hoodie, loudly snapping a piece out of its plastic pocket against the thin metallic seal.

"You want some gum?"

"You know that they've got robots that do surgery now," I answered.

"Doing what, taking gum out of people's hair?" He laughed. "What the fuck, *chotu*. Where the fuck did that come from?"

"No, they've just — they've got these robots. I was reading about them, and it sounds — like in two thousand and one, they did an operation where the dude was in France, and the surgeons were in New York. And that's back then, so you can imagine how far things have come."

"Sure."

"And the two big robots, one of them is called Zeus, and the other one is called Da Vinci. You know what I mean?"

"About what?"

"The, whatever — you know. You know. The king of the gods on the one hand, right, versus the genius of man. And it looks like the Da Vinci, that's the big one. That's the one that they're using all over the States. And you start thinking, '*Yeah*,' you know, '*they're finally taking human beings out of the picture, that's great.*' You know *The Independent*?"

"Robert Fisk's paper?"

"Yeah. They called their story on it 'The Rise of the Machines.' But then *National Geographic* says it's just another tool, and then this other blog says it'll make it so that, like, super experienced old doctors, who aren't as nimble as they used to be, they'll be able to use the machines to sort of, fucking, stay on point. Like the end of *Microserfs*, remember? With the mom? So is it really even getting rid of the people?

I just went back and forth on it for hours, typing in different searches, you know."

We lay for a few long seconds in unimpressed silence, the ambient sounds of the lake once again noticeable, like the lost ticking of a clock returned to a room.

"Daniel," he said finally. "How long are you going to be doing this for?"

"*Birji*," I said, the underside of my jaw already tensing in order to keep me from weeping, "I'm going to go crazy some day. The muscles are going to snap slack and I'll go crazy."

I buried my head in his chest, somehow both warm and cool, as he held the back of my neck in his hands, closing his eyes, neither of us missing anything by way of showers in the blue-black sky.

○

Sara and Nicole's home in Kitsilano is tiny, beautiful, a deep and vibrant blue accented with thick white and strawberry tones around the trim. After a few glasses of wine, my cousin sometimes confesses to me that she worries that Robeson will be too divorced from the family's working class roots, ensconced, as he is, in the easy and beautiful comfort of Kits. Welcome to Vancouver: Where the Sons of Dykes Might Not be Oppressed Enough.

In 1998, Tony and Rose Davis, the owners of the home, had furthered their retreat from the national madness of their country of birth by moving permanently to what had been a summer home on Galiano Island. It marked the culmination of a refuge-taking that had started in 1971, when young Tony had left his Los Angeles home for Vancouver in order to evade the mire of Vietnam. Rose had joined him in 1974, moving back and forth from the Bay Area to Canada's West Coast until Tony's new Canadian citizenship and the death knell of Jesse Jackson's Rainbow Coalition made the move permanent in the late 1980s. With the political climate engendered by special prosecutor Ken Starr's puritanical crusade against the fellated Democratic president in '98, though, the Davis's no longer felt Vancouver provided sufficient shade from the persecutorial radiation of the homeland, and dove further into safety on their wooded property on Galiano.

The move to the island had worked out well for Nicole and Sara, Tony and Rose. The former got to rent a magnificent home for an obscenely reasonable monthly rate, and the latter, safe in their monastic, TV-free existence, hadn't heard about al-Qaeda's attack until September 12.

Getting off the Arbutus bus, I made my way up the street and then down the walkway to a thick and reddish, heavy front door. There, I rang the large, hanging bell next to the wind chimes. As I waited for Sara to answer, I looked over and saw Robeson playing in the yard next door with a little Chinese boy and a pile of toy cars.

"Hey pal," I called out, waving.

"Hi, Uncle Daniel," Robeson yelled back, not looking up from his game. "Moms are fighting," he added.

"What?" I asked, and as I did Sara answered the door with reddened eyes, with the sound of a bedroom door slamming upstairs.

"Hi, honey," she said.

"Jesus, Sara, are you okay?"

"Come in, sweetie."

Sara closed the door behind me as I slipped my shoes off without unlacing. We moved naturally into the kitchen. Sara, faded, seated herself in a slouch and faced me. Above her, there hung a hand-painted wooden sign with each of their three handprints — Nicole's, Sara's and little Robeson's — and the words "Hate is Not a Family Value." For my taste, it's a little earnest.

"What's up? Is this a bad time? Do you still need me to look after Robeson?"

"Yes honey, yes. We're still — We've got to go to this meeting. That's all that's happening, Daniel, it's just the stresses of this whole, just — all of this bullshit."

"What's the meeting for tonight?"

"Have you ever been to The Purple Page?"

"On Davie Street? The gay bookstore? Sure. I think I went there with you guys, no?"

"Probably. Anyway, the political committee at Purple Page is planning a huge demonstration downtown to show support for *Turtledoves* — for Nicole, really, and we've got this preliminary thing tonight. They already assume that we'll have to contend with a counter-demonstration, of course."

"Anytime soon, the demo?"

"No," she said, shaking her head. "No doubt adding to the stress. They want it months from now, early next school year."

"Fuck. Why?"

"Don't get me started. Don — did you meet Don, from the bookstore?"

"I don't think so, no. Not that I can remember, anyhow."

"Anyhow, Don says they've been burned in the past on the censorship stuff, the fights with customs over the porn stuff and the actions they've done. Whatever, he says in the past they've done things on the cheap in terms of planning, and apparently it's blown up in their face, some big brawl with a bunch of homophobes at a picket at Canada Customs."

"Jesus."

"So now, they want the run-up time to build it, raise funds, work the media, get sort of an ad hoc thing beyond the bookstore going, blah blah blah. It's like they've raised complete stasis up to the level of a political principle, it's so fucking ridiculous. Plus, I guess they want it around back to school time."

"That's super frustrating."

"It is, honey. And then earlier this afternoon, Nicole had a bit of an argument with Gurmit, who thinks that the demonstration should be out in Surrey, instead."

"She's probably right," I offered.

"Well," she said, raising her eyebrows conspiratorially and with surrender, "Don't tell Nicole that's what you think. Because I made that mistake three quarters of an hour ago, and I've had to send Robeson over to the neighbour's to play."

"Yeah, I saw him over there. So, what — Nicole flipped out? That's not like her at all, Sara."

"You don't have to tell me that, Daniel."

A door slammed upstairs, echoing loudly against the bleached hardwood of the house, shaking the Maritimes glass art hanging near bay windows stacked with newspapers and magazines. The sounds of quick, sharp, short footsteps upstairs could be heard, translated cloudily through the floor, as another door slammed and Nicole came down the stairs and entered the kitchen.

"Are we ready to go? Hi, Daniel. How about no Kubrick this time, all right?"

"Hi, Nicole," I replied, with all the affection and sincerity that had been missing from her greeting. "I think I can almost guarantee it. How are you holding up?"

"Well," she said, with a pronounced and frustrated exhalation, "I don't really have any choice, do I, Daniel? I pretty much have to hold up. I'm holding myself up."

Sara raised herself from her seat silently. She left the room under the pretence of grabbing a light jacket in order to face the breeze of the mild spring evening. Nicole checked the elements of the stove, swung her keys on her finger and moved out into the foyer and opened the front door.

"Robeson!" she called out to the neighbouring yard. "Time to come back home. Come give your mommy a kiss and get inside with Uncle Daniel."

A few seconds later Robeson padded into the house, the cuffs of his dirty jeans hugging tightly to the ankles of his shoes. He kissed his mothers on their way out the door, and ran into the kitchen where I was sitting to put his arms behind my neck and kiss me on the cheek.

"Hi, Uncle Daniel," he said.

"I didn't think you recognized me."

"What do you mean?"

"When I came in here, I could barely get you to look up."

"Oh, Uncle..." he said, musically. I smiled warmly at

the sight his blasé eight-year-old posture and the larval-ado-
lescent coolness that rang in his voice as he dismissed my
insecurities with a wave of his hand. "That's just because I
was playing with Lukas."

"Yeah? Did you guys have fun?"

"Lukas can be funny but also, sometimes, he's bossy."

"Bossy, huh? Well, I order you never to be bossy, pal."

Robeson laughed, cocking his fists and speaking out of
one side of his little mouth: "I order you to get punched in
the face, pal."

As a big-buddy friend, I would have played along, and
let Robeson harmlessly tease me with innocent violent im-
agery. But after the *Clockwork* debacle, my avuncular responsibility was under closer scrutiny than ever.

"Hey," I said in the long, drawn-out condescension of
a still-cool guardian, "What would your moms say if they
heard you using talk like that, hey buddy?"

"Oh Uncle," he said, waving me off again. "*Mothers just
want always to be gentle.*"

I almost fell off my chair. With clouds of tears already
stinging my eyes, I told Robeson I had to go to the bathroom, rushing up the stairs that Nicole had pounded down
minutes earlier and locking myself into the master bedroom
just as the sobs became uncontrollable. I fell back onto the
bed grabbing my face, holding it hard against my skull so
as not to lose it in the flood of tears borne out by Robeson's
passing reference to maternal softness. *Mothers just want always to be gentle* sounded in my ears and images of me in my
paper mask at Mom's bedside lit a path across my eyes.
Tubes running into the top of the hand she touches my face
with — IV, IV stand — and I fall back several steps in order

not to hurt her with my germs. Pictures of me orphaned, a surprise ending revealed halfway through the first chapter while others my age dealt with early bedtimes.

Robeson knocked on his mothers' door, as I ran into the ensuite, splashing water onto my face in now-familiar ritual, washing the salt out of my eyes and off of my cheeks, calling out for him to *Wait*, that *I'll be right there*.

Robeson looked a lot like Nicole and, though it couldn't have been more than coincidence or wishful thinking, his face even, sometimes, evoked Sara.

When they'd first met, at SFU, Nicole had been in the early stages of her pregnancy, grading English papers and teaching her small tutorial seminar, the subset of an Introduction to Fiction course taught by a popular professor. The teaching assistant position was part of her scholarship package, subsidizing a master's thesis on Queer Themes in Canadian Immigrant Literature.

Sara had, at the time, been studying physics and heterosexuality, failing at both. Taking Introduction to Fiction in order to fill breadth requirements, she was hypnotized by Nicole's searing charisma and confidence, her ease with knowledge, and her wry sarcasm. Stealing quick glances at the outlines of her nipples behind relaxed fabrics during office hours, Sara started visiting Nicole for help with greater and greater frequency.

"Margaret Atwood is like the Gordon Lightfoot of literature," she'd said one day in November, smiling asymmetrically. "Because she's the go-to author for square Canadian nationalists, the tendency of hip people will be to talk shit. Just like with Lightfoot. But just like with Lightfoot, I mean — it's useless to deny the genius. Best to just roll with it."

She had laughed offhandedly, then, as though at someone else's joke. She reached both hands behind her head to fix the bun in her hair, arching herself to the warmly confused delight of her student.

After the course had finished, Sara hadn't heard from Nicole for over a month. Then, out of nowhere, she received a mass email from Nicole's account, asking "friends and comrades" to attend a work-party for CISPI, the "Communities in Solidarity with the People Of Iraq." Eagerly, she'd responded affirmatively to Nicole's invitation, wondering to herself what one ought to wear to a work-party for the Iraqis.

For the first months, Sara's time with Nicole had been outwardly unromantic; time spent mostly leafleting uninterested tourists on Robson Street about international solidarity, then cooing over newborn Robeson. Sara would hold the baby whenever Nicole stood in line for the microphone at public forums, or whisper summaries of missed conversations when she came back into a committee meeting after having left to change a diaper. Whenever she did, she would draw out the descriptions unnecessarily, include every extraneous detail and digression, often repeating herself or feigning poor memory, keeping her mouth close to Nicole's ear.

At night, Sara would writhe sleeplessly and dramatically, trying to plan a cool seduction or a method for confessing her love. She wrote pretend letters to Nicole, stringing together the kinds of maudlin adolescent platitudes that she might have gotten out of her system while a teenager had she not then been so preoccupied with suppressing the waves of nausea that beset her as boyfriends clumsily requested blow jobs with the light application of different kinds of pressure.

She had pined and deliberated, tormenting herself until one night, essentially identical to most others they had spent together, the sexless friendship collapsed under the weight of its tension; an event that mocked all the effort and emotion of her late night meditation and suffering with its sheer simplicity: they put Robeson to bed, walked back into the living room, and fucked until they broke the ornamental ceramic bowl that Nicole had won in a silent auction meant to raise money for the Zapatistas.

Nicole's first book, *Becka's Jobs*, had been put out by a small Vancouver publisher and had sold quite well in the shops and to the crowds for which it had been written by design: the junior-feminist, self-esteem plot guaranteed the interest of a certain, suddenly child-rearing, demographic. In her book, the title character Becka takes her older brother Jeffy, who has insisted stubbornly on the general incapacity of girls for some time, on a colourfully illustrated tour of all the jobs she was capable of one day performing (teacher, doctor, lifeguard, firefighter, scientist, construction worker, news reporter, veterinarian, sea captain, and barista were the potential vocations highlighted, as I remember, and modes of employment which would have been distasteful in the eyes of the progressive audience envisioned for the book — police officer, banker, security guard, logger, movie star — were conspicuously absent).

Nicole had wanted to illustrate the book herself, but Sara had pleaded the case of her friend Brian, a visual artist and illustrator, dying of AIDS and then nearly penniless. A year and a half after the book had been published, Brian died from the complications of a case of pneumonia, and a picture of him hung in the same frame as one of the book's first prints, in the hallway between Robeson's room and his mothers'.

I was doing much better in terms of babysitting this time. Once we'd finished our wholly appropriate movie — with its forgettably loveable animal characters and just enough witty lines aimed over the heads of the younger viewers to earn, in massive, strenuously zany font across the back cover of the DVD case, an inane description as "wild fun for every member of the family" — Robeson settled in a corner of Nicole's cedar coloured office reading comics. I sat at her computer, improvising a little homemade Biomedical Library, doing what's called, in the business, a "grey literature" search: Googling and Yahooing and immersing myself in Wikipedia.

Over the course of a largely incidental search on pacemakers, I followed hyperlinks without focus, listening to Robeson's breathing and wallowing through the material dead-eyed until I came across a June 2005 article from the BBC about a device being used experimentally on patients with depression and OCD. My hand was shaking slightly on the mouse, twitching the cursor, the machine echoing my biology like an inversion of the pacemaker they were describing: the power source sat under the rib-plate, the electrical work shooting along the sides of the throat; the electricity worked to stimulate one lobe while calming the other, and though the thing was made for Parkinson's it seemed maybe it could fix a short-circuiting mind — as though it were sitting in a robot, designed for something useful but backfiring instead, constantly crying or washing its hands. Two thirds of the test subjects were better after a year.

For a few minutes, I sat re-reading the article, touching the screen with my index finger and taking long sips from the powdery, poorly stirred iced tea that I had made for myself while, after the film, Robeson had been eating a bowl of cereal and soy milk. I mouthed the words of the article like a semi-literate, wondering how I felt about the discovery as Robeson piped up from his comics.

"Uncle," he said, as he rose from the floor in his pyjamas and made his way over to my seat. "When's mommies coming home?"

"Soon, sweetie. Soon," I answered absently, still reading the piece. Then, turning my face and attention towards him, I added: "Your mommies are at an important meeting tonight, pal. We might have to put you to bed before they get home. But they'll come wake you up for a kiss when they get back."

Robeson rubbed the base of his palm up against his eyes, yawning.

"What are you reading, Uncle Daniel?"

"Come here," I said, lifting him up onto my knee so that he could see the monitor and the pictures that went along with the piece. Within a year, he'd be too old for me to do that. Maybe he already was.

"Do you know what a 'pacemaker' is, buddy?"

He shook his head, which weighed heavily on his neck and shoulders with want of sleep.

"A pacemaker is a little machine that the doctors put inside your heart to keep it beating properly, so that you can still live if your heart doesn't work right."

"Oh," he said, more in keeping with the script than in

actual interest.

"And these guys in this story have invented a pacemaker that goes in your brain, and uses electricity to make it so that people who are sad all of the time don't have to be. Not just sad, you know, I mean — people who have very serious problems with being sad, so sad that they can't do anything at all. So these guys have invented a machine that goes in their brain." Then, after a small sigh, I told him: "You know the pills that I take, buddy? You remember when I came here to stay for a few days while I took my new medicine?"

"Yeah."

"Well, this machine that they invented for peoples' brains, it's for the same problems that I take my medicine for." Then, unsuccessfully trying to lighten the mood, to free Robeson from the heaviness of my meditation, I added, "Maybe they should turn your uncle into a cyborg."

Robeson touched the screen where a photo of an iridescent brain lit up above a sober caption explaining the procedure.

"That's weird."

"Yeah, it is kind of weird."

"Yeah, it's weird."

"But why do *you* think that it's weird, buddy?"

"Well, because if those guys put electricity into somebody's brain, if he got his head in the water he would get electrocuted."

"Yeah," I said, suppressing a smile. "I don't think they have to worry about that so much, sweetie."

"Electricity can't go in water or else it becomes electrocution."

"That's true, Robeson, but these doctors are so smart

that they know how to make it so that none of the water can ruin the electricity from the machines."

"Oh," he said. "That's pretty smart."

"Yes. But a lot of people might think that this is weird because, you know — They think that it's a person's brain that makes them special, and that their thoughts and their feelings are sacred, and that a machine like this is wrong because it changes what goes on in people's minds."

"Uncle Daniel, what's 'sacred'?"

"It means very, very special."

"Oh." Then: "Do you think it's a bad machine, Uncle?"

"I'm not sure, pal. I don't know what I think about it. I know your mom would hate it, that's for sure. Your mommy Sara, my cousin, would not like it at all. But I think it's complicated, bud. Like, for hundreds and hundreds of years, people thought that it was your *heart* that created your feelings, that your heart was what made you special."

"Was hearts sacred?"

"Yes, they were very sacred. More sacred than brains. Way more sacred. So if you were to go back in time even a hundred and fifty years, and say to someone 'We're going to make two pacemakers, we're going to make two machines, one to control your heart and another to control your brain,' which do you think they'd think was worse?"

"The brain," Robeson replied with confidence.

"No, I think it would be the heart, buddy."

An hour later, before his mothers had come home, Robeson fell asleep on the loveseat. His comics were underneath him, crumpled past any potential for accumulating value. I made my way down into the kitchen, opened the cupboard, and wondered what possible difference from regular corn nuts could be manifested in their organic counterparts as I poured myself a small bowl out of an expensive-looking bag thereof and thumbed the number to Bo's cell into Sara and Nicole's cordless phone.

"Bo Grewal," he answered, using his caller ID in order to ascertain that I — the person who hated the method of using one's name to answer one's phone perhaps more than anyone else in the world — was the one calling from my cousin's lesbian palace in Kits.

"Hi," I responded, enunciating wildly, and pronouncing his family name like the food dolloped out to orphans. "Is *Bo Grew-al* there, please?"

"What's up?"

"You want to pick me up in a bit? Let's go for a coffee or something." Then, running my tongue back onto itself, feeling sugar-sensitive tastebuds destined to remain unexercised by the bowl of organic corn nuts: "Fuck it. Let's go get some dessert, yo."

"You want to go to the Naam?" Bo asked. His suggestion was sincere, but with the requisite levels of irony to indicate the component of contempt in his love/hate relationship with Vancouver's cliché-ridden, twenty-four hour orgy of vegetarian fare.

"Do you remember that massage parlour that used to be across the way from the Naam?"

"The Tokyo Health Sauna or whatever? The one that Jimmy Tan went to for his birthday?"

"Yes."

"What about it?"

"It's a baby supplies store, now," I said gleefully, crunching toasted corn between my molars, drowning out whatever reply Bo might have mustered. "What?"

"I said I'll be there in forty-five minutes."

"*Sat sri akal ji.*"

"*Sat sri akal.*"

As I hung up with the same thumb with which I'd dialed, I heard keys turning in the lock of the front door. I bolted to the doorway to keep them quiet, to let them know that Robeson was sleeping on the couch and could easily be woken up. I arrived in the foyer just in time to see Nicole, tear-streaked and trembling, push past decorum on the way up to their bedroom. Sara entered the house a few steps behind.

"Jesus, Sara," I said. "This shit is killing her."

"Not if it kills me first, sweetie."

○

Bo and I rode in silence for a few minutes before he piped up, backing his car into a parallel parking spot open across from the Naam, in front of the rehabilitated whorehouse.

"I've been thinking about something you said a few weeks ago," he intoned slyly, "about *Turtledoves.*"

"Oh yeah?"

"Yeah."

"What's that?"

"Do you remember how you said — Like, when you were telling me about the whole thing and you, remember, you emphasized that there was nothing sexual at all about the book?"

"Right."

"Well, I was thinking about that the other night while I

was watching this stand-up comic on TV." We were sitting, now, in the parked car, watching the lineup in which we'd soon be standing lengthen every few seconds as it snaked out the door. "This comic — he goes, 'Which do you think you'd less like to see your father wearing? A cock ring or a toe ring? Which one would make you more uncomfortable?'"

"Hm," I said, smiling.

"Because the answer, actually, is toe ring."

"You think?"

"Absolutely. Absolutely. It's — the frightening thing to people about gays — It's never been about sexual preference in the end, I don't think. I mean shit, you're the Marxist, not me, but it seems to me that it's easy enough to get around the psychological and religious debris, the bullshit. It's not so hard to conceive of, even, say, a straight guy who gets off on the idea of a cock in his hands or some shit, getting hit or bossed around?"

"Okay."

"Let me start this again. I've told you before, you know, that I think my dad knows I go to bed with white girls."

"Yes, I remember — "

"The point is, even though he knows that his son isn't a twenty-eight-year-old virgin — I mean he knows but he doesn't, right — but he knows that I've gone to bed with somebody and he also knows that if he hasn't seen the girls I'm going to bed with, then it's likely that I'm hiding them for a reason."

"Because they have cat's eyes."

"Exactly. Because they have cat's eyes. But I don't think that it bothers him. Shit, he might be proud of me planting the flag. The point is, between the sheets, I'm not disrupting anything social. The only time I'm going to catch a smack from his direction sex-wise is when I show up trying to marry anybody other than a *jatt*, Sikh, Punjabi."

"Right, okay."

"These same assholes," he continued, "who hate the idea of *Turtledoves* so much, they're paying twenty bucks a shot for *Girls Gone Wild* videos full of sorority girls licking each other's tongues and fingering each other's pussies. But with those smooth, blonde bitches — I mean, you know that none of them is going to do anything but end up married, making kids, and letting the memories of sucking her roommate's earlobes fade under however many Republican votes, right? But they won't stop reproducing a workforce. They won't let the fact that they kissed a girl in front of a camera at Mardi Gras keep them from taking orders from men for the rest of their lives."

"And so *Turtledoves*..."

But Bo was on a roll. "*Turtledoves*," he pressed on, "gets at something scarier. The living together, the strident freedom of it, this rejection of one of their very simplest rules, you know? This thing that's supposed to be a given?" He stopped short, changing track, still fogging up the insides of the car righteously, but now with a message he felt confident in making explicitly and specifically about me. "See, what it *is* is that they pretend to be afraid about what's happening with people's bodies, but in the end it comes down to what's going through their minds. And with you, it's the opposite."

I sat mutely staring over his shoulder. The growing line of hippies and cash-laden bohemians poured out of the Naam onto the 4th Avenue sidewalk as Bo repeated himself.

"You see what I mean, man? With you, it's the opposite. You pretend to be afraid of what happens to the mind, when actually — "

"I don't understand," I said finally, "how we went from talking about Nicole's book to this — "

"I just think, you know, that I've been on eggshells with this thing, and it's not what I ought to be doing, as a friend. This whole thing. Enough already, you know? It's not helping you, so I'm trying to. "

"By what? By equating me with the fucking hicks and puritans who are killing my cousins with their — "

"I'm not equating you with them, Daniel. Jesus! What did I just say? I said with you it was the *opposite*. "

"I think I know what you're saying, Bo."

"No," he sounded, emphatically. "No, *Chotu*, I do not think that you understand what I'm trying to say. The body, the mind, the machines — it's like you're trying to project trauma off enough surfaces that it loses — "

"I mean is this some kind of intervention?"

"Sure. *Fine*. Call it that. I tried to keep my mind open about the whole thing. At the beginning, you know, I even thought it was commendable, the autodidactic thing. But then it started to turn, you know, and I think I only really started to process what bothered me about it at the meteor shower."

"*Birji*," I said, hoping that the honorific would soften the edges of what was quickly becoming far too intense and accurate a scrutiny for my comfort. "I was stoned."

He shook his head, resigned, sighing "*Daniel*." A muted ambulance siren skirted the edges of earshot with a dullness that sharpened as the vehicle drew closer, slowing momentarily at the intersection of Macdonald and 4th before pouring past the hippie lineup and the fogging the Jetta in which Bo and I sat.

"You know, when I was a kid," I started softly, following the ambulance for a few seconds with my eyes and neck and shoulders, trying unsuccessfully to make it out through the thick, wet grey now lining the insides of the car's windows, "I used to have to say a prayer every time I heard a siren. I had to pray that it wasn't for anyone that I knew, because if I didn't, and it turned out to be, it would be my fault. Then I had to end the prayer in a very specific, you know, sort of routine way. I thought I was religious, Bo. I said 'Lord, please don't let that siren be for anyone that I know, Lord, please. I love you God, Amen.' And then, over the course of a few months, maybe a year, a whole, compulsive postscript cropped up, after 'Amen.' I would single out Christ, my mother, that little kid — do you remember those two ten-year-old boys in England, and they kidnapped that two year old from the mall, and took him to the railroad tracks and –"

"I do remember that. And they said — like, not the kids, but the journalists and doctors and whoever, they said that it was from watching the Chucky movies."

"*Child's Play.* That's right. Well, that kid, the kid that they killed, I singled him out, too. I'd name these people by name and ask God to take care of them in Heaven, because I felt that they were my responsibility."

"How old would you have been when this was going on?"

"Maybe eleven, twelve."

"Fuck."

"And, of course, nobody knew — "

"That it was OCD."

"I just thought I was religious. I joined the youth group at church, but whenever we would go anyplace, all I could think of was sex." I laughed. "We went swimming once and I spent the whole time trying not to get caught staring at the outlines of the pubic hair underneath this girl Patricia's bathing suit. What I'm saying is, you know, praying six or seven times an hour or not, I don't think I was ever too religious."

Bo smiled weakly, looking at the blank canvas of windshield in front of him, tapping his huge knuckles, with their long, manly black hairs, on the thighs of his jeans. He'd taken his stand, reached out to help a very dear friend in the process of asphyxiating himself in isolating texts, of mounting a live burial in the library basement with its phagocyte graffiti and, instead of gratitude, the suffocating friend had offered an irrefutable, poor-me soliloquy as a means of defusing the ardour of his saviour. Like a castaway firing a flare at the chest of a rescue pilot.

Satisfied with the cruelty of my victory, I touched Bo on the shoulder, a consolation and, pretending to shift the balance of power, asked: "Let's go in. Some sesame fries?"

"*Tikka*," he said, with a damp and vanquished breath.

○

If there's a problem with excessive masturbation, it's got nothing to do with preserving sight or saving souls. As a numb ache laced the tiny bones of the hand and wrist that I had wrapped around my genitals, hunched over my computer and coming at the sight of women I wouldn't have looked twice at on the bus, I considered the fact that nothing — with the possible exception of the obsessive rumination of OCD — reinforced my uncompromised solipsism more than masturbation to excess. So I guess it's kind of about saving souls. But not in any way that Pastor Gerry would recognize.

What struck me most when I read Nelson Mandela's autobiography — a Christmas gift from Sara, Nicole, and Robeson — was the degree to which the first-person singular easily submerged and reappeared, dissolved and crested against the panoramic background of collectivity, struggle. This traumatized society in absolute upheaval against absolute suppression, drowned the individual with bureaucratic terms like "Bantu" and then opened fire across the young spines at Soweto. So did Mandela masturbate on Robben Island? To try to answer misses the point: I think it's tacky as shit to ask in the first place.

But I think prison and masturbation share a crossroads: the explosive borderland where the body and the mind choose either to part or to subsume each other. The best-case scenario in each is that the mind possesses itself of this absolute freedom that sublimates the needs, desires, pains, pleasures, and horrors of the corporeal. Bars, fences, barbed wire, irons, keys, and bricks step in as the physical and mechanical application of the mind's imperatives for the body, just like crutches or a dildo.

But there are whole armies of catalogue-shoppers and men with golf shirts tucked in to their pants who take Mandela's transcendence as a cue, perverting it into a sort of late-capitalist subjectivism where the mind, as expressed by will power, is all that exists. After all, the founding ideal of liberalism is the individualist cult built around *cogito ergo sum* (plus all the attendant clichés that crop up in the vernacular as a result: *it's the thought that counts, mind over matter*), and this makes me wonder if OCD isn't just the terrible culmination of a pathological interplay between ego and images that we try to pass off as a society. When I was a kid my uncle once asked, as a joke, "Why do guys get a lighter sentence for attempted murder than they do for murder? He's still trying to kill the guy, he just didn't pull it off." As though we could do that, build a whole judicial system on hidden thoughts, shadowed intentions — intentions that maybe even the perpetrator doesn't realize he has. From an early age, I knew I couldn't separate action from intention philosophically, and so I was crippled.

How am I different, except by degree, from the woman who won't let her kids watch the news, because the images of war inflict too much pain? We both put a greater-than sign between our minds and the world. This, I wanted to tell Gary, is why I could never be a good commie. Who could read the *German Ideology* and still be an obsessive-compulsive?

So, in the end, it isn't my furious wanking to the material on a website whose domain name I couldn't possibly share that casts me as the disfigured shadow of Mandela's platonic humanity — it's that my biography is just a sketch, an extended self-absorption, a POV narrative, in a way totally unlike Sara's, or Nicole's, or even Gary's. The world is just the place where I live.

Drying myself off with my boxers, I picked up a copy of an ancient, pocket medical dictionary that I'd bought in a used bookstore back when I was still so unburdened by knowledge that I thought a book of medical practices and terms published in the late 1950s would still be of use. In the beginning, I would lie back on my bed, beneath the framed picture of Che Guevara, and leaf through the yellowed, aromatic pages of the small, reddish book. My favourite page was buried in the H's: homoplasty, homopolysaccharide, homorganic, homosexuality, homostimulant.

I closed the book before putting it on my nightstand. Beneath the hot lamp that I turned off in the same motion, I smiled and hoped that in the following editions of the dictionary, no new words had come about to separate the medical condition of homosexuality from the perversely innocent "homostimulant." I turned over and began to fall asleep within minutes. Just before sleep took me, though, in the hypnagogic dusk when half-lucid chimera fade into night dreams, it occurred to me that Che had been a medical doctor. I thought of Norman Bethune, and of Huey P. Newton selling little red books: my desiccated old medical dictionary. Eldridge Cleaver would have ripped out the pages on homoplasty.

O

In the earliest days of my study, I hadn't even the advantage of *Dorland's*, and used regular dictionaries, both the online and dust-covered, looking up any words that tripped me. Wanting to add a dimension of specificity to my understanding of a particular piece relating to dermatology, I had sought out "pore":

**pore: (1) | noun**
a minute opening in a surface, through which
gases, liquids and particles can pass. ORIGIN late
middle English: from Old French, via Latin from
Greek *poros. "passage, pore"*

And the second definition which, to me, didn't seem
altogether unconnected:

**pore: (2) | verb**
to be absorbed in the reading or studying of: *She
spent hours poring over her book.*
•ARCHAIC to think intently on, to ponder: *He
ruminated a long while; he thought and pored over it.*
ORIGIN Middle English: Perhaps related to
**PEER.**

It was the last point that had tripped me up: *peer*. I realize now that they meant to look, to peer at something. But
for the longest time I thought it came from the other *peer* —
a contemporary, part of a cohort. Somebody in the same
boat as me. And that's why, at first, the two definitions had-
n't seemed to be so different. A peer, a contemporary, to
whom I might have been connected through our own
minute openings, passages.

# VII

The two weeks in the Psych Ward were cobwebs now, sitting rather than milling in the back of Ty's memory as he pushed up Commercial Drive, past the antiques near Venables, towards the apartment he'd been renting for three months up near Donald's Market, just across from the Van East cinema, ever since he'd gotten back from LA. As he passed the veteran's memorial at Grandview Park, beside which hippies played hacky sack and read Tarot cards seven months of the year, Ty thought about how quickly it had gone from just playing with the knife and thinking about it to an actual cut. There had been none of the poetry he'd hoped for, only that deep and maudlin cut. The doctors had made that clear, telling Ty daily that it hadn't been the romance of an existential crisis, as he'd imagined. Triggers. Everything, for these people, was just a trigger setting off a chemical imbalance that was already there, a seeping darkness in the brain's myriad crevices and folds, a lack of electricity or serotonin or whatever sort of lack. To them, it was all just physiology lying in wait to manifest itself psychologically. An attempted suicide due not at all to what he'd thought had caused it, that hollow emptiness that had overtaken him when Sampson walked onstage at the Emmys and waved, and all he could do was cry. The realization that everything that had happened was just an inversion of Sampson's misery, that Ty had come to define his own success in the terms set exclusively by another man's atrophy; his only peak had been the valley in a life he was living far beneath.

The whole world was rooting for Sampson, at each incremental step towards wellness: when he came to, out of the coma, still held in place by the cast, and then all through the therapy that gave him back his faculties; the *People* magazine cover with wife Lynn holding Sampson across his chest from behind her seated husband, Sampson managing a weak smile out of the corner of his mouth, a new beard grown in to cover most of the scarring; the medical professionals swooning over the near-miraculous speed of his recovery, gushing lines about laughter being the best medicine that the magazines could use as pull quotes. And the healthier he got, the more tasteless Ty had seemed wearing Sampson's headphones, reading scripts into the studio mic on Wednesdays and Thursdays. More and more cast outings went by without invitations — dinners and birthday parties at which Sampson started to appear, first in a chair, then with crutches, finally with a cane. At Josh Stern and his young wife's fifth anniversary party, Sampson had been the guest of honour, drawing sympathy, laughter, and pleas for a quicker return.

"Al — when are you coming back, man? It's just not the same without you," and Ty didn't even register who it was who had said it — given the sentiment, it could have been anybody there — just that it had been said, that it had been said next to him, that there wasn't even a moment of awkwardness that followed, so evident was it that all the cast and writers and producers and directors and audience wanted Al to come home and Ty to be sent back to his impressions and low-ceilinged comedy clubs, restaurants converted weekly into performance halls, half-filled with patrons unaware that there would be comedy and unwilling to lower voices thrown fulsomely into conversation. Al had smiled, run his knuckles along Debbie Hunting's cheek, and said, to raucous laughter, "I'll be home soon, my pets" in an exaggerated Vincent Price.

And this had been what Ty told the doctors, stitches itching across the inside of his forearm, so high up from the wrist that the scar wouldn't look to anyone else like attempted suicide: he'd suddenly realized that he was a void, a human negative instead of a positive — in fact the most intricate and understanding notion that he'd ever managed in his life, his greatest introspection, had been the damning midnight impulse to go from grazing the knife against himself to plunging, gouging. The doctor had frowned, nodding his head patronizingly, easing Ty into the knowledge that *We don't really look for those sorts of answers anymore*, as though Ty had come in explaining his suicide in terms of penis envy, as though he'd asked the doctor to stroke a goatee and analyze his dreams. They tried to let him know that that kind of psychology had fossilized, disappeared like auto industry jobs, faith in progress, housewives in aprons. These things were now mostly pharmacological matters. What he had taken to be an existential crisis was merely a trigger for a major depressive episode, not a subterranean explanation for his actions.

But triggers still had to be pulled to do what he'd tried, so that's what he laid out in the letter he'd written. There, in the suicide note, jotted down like one of his nebulous joke ideas, the existential analysis worked. It moved the story into the newspaper, one last wave of notoriety to carry him back into stand-up, give him a gimmick to take to the clubs. The nut, the anti-Sampson. Guy who tried to off himself, feeling so small for drawing all his light from the shadow cast by a superstar's brush with death, and now he's doing Kermit the Frog impressions, Bill Cosby, Christopher Walken. *Casting a movie is important man, I'm telling you. You don't believe me? Like Oliver Stone's JFK, right? Great movie. But what if, instead of Joe Pesci, he'd used William Shatner, you know what I mean?* "*Bones ... I... need you to ... beam me ...into ... the Bay of ... Pigs.*" "*Damnit, Jim, I'm a doctor, not a Cuban!*"

"Write a book," his double-chinned and poorly dressed Vancouver agent, Carl, had insisted, spitting lightly as he spoke in the Gastown offices two blocks insulated from the AIDS and drugs and static malaise of the Downtown East-side. After *Army Brats*, his Canadian management had re-gained its primacy. "Or let's get one written for you, get a ghostwriter, put something together — 'I stood in for Al Sampson,' you know, that's interesting stuff. Nice hard-cover, do a little tour starting here, LA, Toronto, maybe New York, for sure Chicago. You could even do Edmonton. It'll be, it's a nice — funny stuff on the set, insights behind the scenes. That sort of thing could do very well in the States, get your name out, and we start booking some shows. Some corporates. Mike," he had said, gesturing down the hall, suggesting with the antenna of his cellphone a space through the glass wall of his own office, "Mike's done plenty of literary stuff. Hell, I'll cut him in on my end. And then, that's out there, and you're out there, you know, and it works."

Ty had taken a long sip of tea from the plastic mug brought by the young secretary Carl shared with Mike and two other agents on the same floor. She had blue highlights in her hair, and smiled kindly at Ty when she brought him his drink.

"Earl Grey?" she'd said, posing the announcement as a question, the volcanic force of twenty-two years of ladylike upbringing pushing the end of each of her sentences upwards.

"Earl Grey for the Duke of Earl," Carl had added moronically, before singing "Duke-Duke-Duke Duke of Earl-Earl-Earl," and then drumming on his desk with his thumbs in order to cover up the silence.

"A ghostwriter?" Ty asked.

"Somebody to write the book. You're still the author, it's your name, you shape the thing, but somebody else does the heavy lifting. Essentially, we get somebody in here to interview you, throw something together, you know, somebody experienced, and then you're out there. You've got a book."

"Sounds about right."

Now moving up the Drive, Ty stepped aside as an elderly Native woman with braids and a scooter passed by him, an upside-down Canadian flag hanging from behind her seat. Two Chinese girls, teenagers, no more than five paces behind her made their ways laughing northbound down the sidewalk, sharing a cellular phone and the reflection of sunlight from their braces. Ty passed Abruzzo, one of the neighbourhood's dozens of Italian cafés in which old men played cards in back rooms and spoke loudly on the streets, eyeing girls of varying ethnicities, women whose male counterparts cheered for different soccer teams than the old men did. Stopping to tie his shoe, Ty leaned against a beige brick column, and caught the whiff of vegetarian cooking from the Café du Soleil, owned by the same family that ran the nearly homophonous Café Deux Soleils up the street. He turned slowly, facing the window display of the People's Co-Op Bookstore, the Communist Party's bookshop, in which was featured prominently an article from the *People's Voice* newspaper defending free speech in the case of *Turtledoves*. A new school year was about to start and still no decisions had been made. The book itself accompanied the cut-out. Ty smiled and stepped into the shop.

"Afternoon," said the tall, thin man hunched over the desktop computer at the till, his fingers as long as his silver ponytail.

Ty nodded, moving over towards the children's section, picking up *Turtledoves*, remembering the gay guy who had flipped out on him that night at Brew Meadows, the massive Sikh following the indignant little white man out onto the street, into the salt air coming off the beach and mixing with Kits's satays and lattes. He flipped through the book, looking mostly at the pictures, fairly compelling despite, or maybe because of, their cartoonishness.

He replaced *Turtledoves* and moved through the store, casually imagining his own book on the shelf across from the cash register upon which sat new releases in hardback. Next to the cashier sat a plastic box filled with voodoo doll likenesses of right-wing politicians, filled with catnip. *Rich people sic their dogs on you,* thought Ty, smiling. *And poor people throw you to their cats. I ought to sell that joke to Chris Mariner.*

Beside the shelf of new releases was a wall filled with books by local authors.

"Jesus," Ty said out loud, accidentally, retroactively addressing his bewilderment to the cashier. "I didn't know there were so many books from Vancouver."

"Sure," said the man with the long hands, long hair.

"Yeah?"

"Mm."

*Is this where you'll put my book?* Ty smirked, then smiled. *What if the ghostwriter is from Toronto?*

# VIII

Since the bone marrow transfusion, Gary had been back to Halifax several times, warming slightly more about his brother before and after each trip, telling stories about the Party days, before the split, and then rushing to describe, again, the violent vomiting that had accompanied the anaesthetic. He would leave, for two or three weeks at a time, having amalgamated the kind of seniority and bank of sick days and holidays that a man like him would never have caught up with in the absence of some trauma.

There was a new colour to his face when he had come downstairs before his most recent departure. He'd come in with a bottle of wine from Chile, and we'd drunk it from water glasses at my kitchen table. He played with a copy of the previous week's *Georgia Straight*, which had been lying unread on my table since it was new.

"You know, you wouldn't believe how much more radical this paper was when it got started. Did you know that about the *Straight*?"

"Sure," I'd answered. "Yeah, sure."

He sat for a few moments longer, batting the paper between his hands like a slow game of pinball.

"Ah, what the hell," he said, unprompted. "Who the hell am I? I guess they still carry a lot of useful stuff." After we'd finished two thirds of the bottle, we'd taken turns at failing to fit the cork back into the bottle. Finally, I'd trotted into the kitchen, fetching a Ziploc and fitting it over the aperture. Gary said I could keep the rest of the bottle, and I thanked him, and he used my phone to call a cab to the airport.

I worried about his brother when I saw a message from Gary in my email a week later. He hadn't titled it, either whimsically or practically. The subject line wasn't quite empty. The word "none" was held between brackets — and that was something altogether more alarming, eerie in the same way as a letter without a return address.

Dear Daniel,

I knew that one day, being a landlord would catch up with me. "What the bourgeoisie produces, above all, is its own gravediggers." I got in trouble because of you last night, Daniel. Well, over you. Rosa laid into me.

We were over at Travis's, and he was sleeping. He sleeps so much. Rosa was making me some peppermint tea. She makes fun of me for leaving Commercial Drive for herbal tea, but she knows how much it comforted me after the transfusion and so she's always got it in her head to make me the stuff. Rosa's partner was an alkie, I don't know if I ever told you; don't see why I would have. Point is, I'm just as happy to have something dry to drink around her, even if I'd rather be sharing one of our bottles of wine.

Somehow — I think it was because she had mentioned the *Turtledoves* story, which she had read about just this week on the Web, and I know that that's your sister's book — we got to talking about you, and your project. Your medical, technological research. Your version of commodity fetishism.

To be honest I was laughing at it, asking Rosa, How could somebody get Marx so wrong? What is there to be gained in such a heartless application of his theory? Marx wanted us to UNDERSTAND our humanity by recognizing our technological, productive capabilities, not ESCAPE it. That's exactly part of what makes us human rather than animal. I cited Engels's essay, "The Part Played by Labour in the Transition from Ape to Man," then I laughed and said you were monkeying around. I got carried away and I was needling Rosa for a response, and I kept pushing at your expense. Said things like you were only interested in "gorilla tactics," that you "must be bananas." I don't know where the malice came from, Daniel, and I'm sorry to have been a bully behind your back. And I'm sorry the jokes were so terrible, too. Talk about an infantile disorder.

You had a ready defender in Rosa, though. She slammed her cup down on Travis's coffee table, stormed out of the room, and slammed the bedroom door. After calling out to her a few times, then staring at my feet for another minute, I followed her down the hall and let myself into the room.

She was livid. Crying, sure, but dry, angry tears.

Vicious. She tore into me good, Daniel, told me I was mocking you as a surrogate for Travis and me. She eviscerated me, pointing out that I hadn't spoken to my little brother in twenty years — that I might never have if he hadn't been dying (she said "dying," which chilled me) and she said that there hadn't been anything human about my socialism since the Rosenbergs, which was an exaggeration. Then she told me to shove my peppermint tea up my ass.

My sister was right, but I think I was too, about your research. My head is spinning. Honestly, I don't know.

I want you to read something, Daniel, because I think it goes a long way to showing what's inhuman, what's too cold about burying your head in the study of machines in order to move away from real human pain. It's an article called 'Dying for Basic Care,' and it was forwarded to me on a progressive list-serve that I'm on. It's from the Washington Post which, as you probably know, was the newspaper that broke the Watergate story (though these days it is quite neo-conservative).

I've posted you the link at the bottom of this message. Essentially, the piece outlines an academic study of how almost a million Blacks died in the United States over the course of the 1990s in deaths that wouldn't have occurred if they'd had access to the same health care as whites. It's a staggering number, obviously, but it's thrown into even sharper relief by the same study's estimate that improving treatment prevented less than two-hundred thousand deaths. In other words, making the technology better saved a fifth the number of people that would have been saved by basic equality.

So, what's the point? I just think this is what happens when we get to thinking about tools as though they had some kind of dialectical dynamism of their own. That there's some idealized space where perfect technology exists divorced from its relationship to human beings and their needs. I know you're imagining that distinction for very different reasons, but still.

There's no world of machines beyond us. It's all still *us*. We made the machines to address our needs. For good or bad, and we're responsible for them. The technologies are FROM us, and they come back around TO us. But the science fiction fantasy that they're above us somehow, or away from us, is just that. In the ice age, that spear WAS our mammoth's tusk.

Are you familiar with the infrastructure-superstructure debate? I know that, as a Marxist, there's a definite side that I'm supposed to be coming down on. But looking at all this, I don't know that I've pulled it off right.

Although I suppose that, as an owner of property, it was just a matter of time before I became a petty bourgeois revisionist.

All the best,
Gary

I quickly followed the link and read the piece, then copied and pasted the text into a blank Word document and requested fifty copies from my printer. Too stunned to cry, I stood and waited as the machine spat out five, fifteen, twenty-five, forty, fifty copies, and I smoothly slipped into my flip-flops while grabbing a roll of masking tape from the top of my dresser. I walked outside, forgetting to lock my door, tripping the sensor light into flooding the pathway darkened by evening's dialectical evolution into night (*stop it!*), and with night, feeling the chill brought to my sockless feet.

Plastering the street with the *Post* article seemed so instinctive, reflexive, that I didn't even think about it. My mind immediately moved from reading and processing the new information to working out postering schedules and routes. Tonight, I would do Commercial from First to Venables, then up by the Cultch theatre and onto Victoria Drive. Tomorrow, I would take the bus to Main Street and King Edward, hit the coffee shops orbiting their mother, the Grind, and maybe even make my way to Cambie Street in order to hit the bougie neighbourhood around the Park cinema and the specialty video stores. The next day, before work, I could get to Kits, do a length of West Broadway and even down to Fourth. I'd have all the time that I would normally have spent with the websites and journals. The awful tearing screech of the tape faded against the traffic and the missionary importance of sharing this news of social, not mechanical, emergency. But how come? Would this kind of news even shock anybody? Weren't my Canadian neighbours already inoculated against this sort of story by grace of their cherished moral superiority over the superpower whose corn syrup and cinema they consumed daily but whose racism they lived to deride? I mean, those are the two things we most love shaking our heads about here: the way the Americans treat blacks and hospitals. Fuck it. *I'll get the stats on Natives in Canada,* I thought. *Or English-French. Think about Royal Victoria in Montreal, compared to the clinic outside of Mononc' Ghislain's place in Drummondville where I got my stitches the summer before Grade Nine.* The broad brushstrokes of what I imagined would be the pyramid of Canada's medical apartheid formed in my head: *Indians at the bottom, the rural French or rural anybody, then citified Anglos. Immigrants someplace, too. Jesus,* I thought, breathing faster, the ridiculousness of taping printed copies of foreign news onto telephone poles suddenly striking me with a sickness in the sides of my stomach. *What impulse is this? Commandante Che? Or is this Dr. Guevara?*

I didn't make it to Venables. At Grandview Park I fell onto a bench beside the children's play area, where a young couple was supervising their two young kids, giving me a slightly suspicious nod as I arranged the thirty-five or so remaining copies of the article in my hands, and then anchored them under my right thigh. For a second, I surrendered myself to the relief of having finished my medical research.

◯

"So how have things been since the last time we met? It's been almost three weeks, I think, since we last checked in," she said, eyes on her computer screen, scrolling. "Never mind this," she said, as she did every time, "just wanted to check where we'd left off."

"They've been okay, for the most part, I guess. I would say, like, medium to high-ish frequency of bad thoughts. I don't know, my mood has been pretty low over the last few days."

"So what's going on?"

"Nothing too special or whatever. Nothing that's — I guess I also had sort of a weird episode last night. I don't know if you'd call it a panic attack or what, but it was a really ... I got *manic*, I would say ...." I trailed off, though I abhorred any conversational vacuum. I was always unwilling, in the doctor's office, to stop talking. Sitting across from her, the searching and sophisticated eye contact, the calendar turned invariably to the page of an incorrect month — there's something in that formula that rushes me to fill any silence. I pull useless old words like coins and Kleenexes from the pockets of unwashed jeans and pile this debris and detritus in front of her in the hopes that she'll cut me off. No place else am I this aware of the vibrations that speech sends through the chest and neck, though in fairness, I drop my voice here to sound less helpless. Today, the monologue gushes with even less form, until finally, plunging into the porridgey slop of space-filling words and pauses, I find the hard kernel of what I wanted to tell her: "I was scared."

"Okay, Daniel. We're just going to — let's back up and go over what exactly happened." Dr. Poitras had been meeting with me long enough to suss out the significance of most of the moods and cadences with which I presented her, had seen the way I rushed to fill the room's conversational space, spinning what are sometimes, in fact, minor worries into speeches that amplify shadows of feeling and worry, swelling them to parade-float caricature. She knows when to assume a firmer stewardship of the session.

It had never been enough of an authority for my liking, though. Never strong or charismatic enough, and that's not because she's a woman. In my case, a female doctor would, in fact, have even greater potential for Oz-like and mystifying projections of power, but she doesn't do it, because she knows that my particular neurosis tweaks for nothing more than a hard-surfaced certainty and last-word reassurance. When I first came to her, following the email address at the end of a local-colour article in the paper about free treatment as part of an OCD study, I simply wanted her opinion on what my thoughts meant: Did I have the potential for violent outburst, as suggested by the wincing snapshots of bloodshed running the loop in my mind's eye? Wouldn't it be easier — rather than scanning myself for slight, inappropriate ticks and nascent arousal whenever kids were around — to simply ask a doctor, point-blank: Am I a paedophile? You studied this shit: Should I be kept away from children? Once-hidden questions took shape in my throat, became spoken, and became heard things. And I wanted, in response to my honesty, authoritative declarations reaffirming what I suspected despite the thoughts: *No, you have no welling violence in you. No, you are no paedophile. Yes, I would let you babysit my children.*

And in the beginning, she told me all those things. She was didactic, using the large whiteboard behind her desk, fully inhabiting the professorial potential of her dark suits and crowded bookshelves, teaching me the differences between the anxieties of the obsessive-compulsive and those of evil-doers (*Paedophiles don't worry about whether they're paedophiles, Daniel, they worry about being caught*) and explaining that these thoughts only illuminated my nature by inversion (*You ruminate over these violent thoughts because you so abhor violence and predation that they have the power to horrify you — that's why none of my atheist patients have blasphemous obsessions*). At first, the conversations were comforting, but her reassurances had no *stay* to them. The sentiments registered ephemerally, raising my spirits for the bus ride home. At least, until some mother got on with her kid, or a wheelchair at an intersection seemed poised to roll into traffic, and I started worrying again about whether I was the worst person in the world. I couldn't wait to see the doctor again and be given moral clearance with absolute surety, backed with a Ph.D. pedigree.

Instead, the reassurances stopped. According to Poitras, my reassurance-seeking had become a compulsion, and had to stop. In a firm voice, she reminded me that we weren't in a confessional booth; the doctor practises what's called "cognitive behavioural therapy," which means that she thinks my OCD can be treated, ameliorated, maybe cured, by changing aspects not only of how I think, but of how I act—superstructure as well as infrastructure. Suddenly, the old questions would be met with *Well, what do you think?* rather than a professional opinion, and I'd clench my teeth to keep the cussing from the air, lifting and pounding my heel against the floor as my knee jackhammered my frustration in improvised Morse code, because if I fucking knew what I fucking thought I wouldn't fucking be here, so please, please, please, please, please.

"My landlord sent me an email, and — and there was a bunch of stuff in it, it's not important, but he linked to this news article about race and inequality of health care in the

States, and for some reason I decided that I had to print it off and go put it up all over town. Like, print off a bunch of copies, and then go tape them up, and I actually did it. As in, I printed off fifty pages of this article, fifty copies, and I left the house. I mean I didn't even lock the door."

"Okay, were you having any trouble breathing?"

"No."

"Dizzy? Heart racing?"

"I'm not sure. I guess I was breathing a bit harder, so I'm sure my heart was racing a bit. But nothing too crazy, I guess."

"Yeah, I don't think you were having a panic attack. With a panic attack — "

"I'm not doing my research anymore," I said suddenly. "I mean ... I'm sorry, I shouldn't have interrupted."

"No, go ahead," she said, with genuine patience. She kept her eyes on mine as she sipped from a silver can of diet pop.

"This news article that I was posting, it seemed to me to indicate that the technological advancements themselves weren't the most important thing for keeping people alive. I shouldn't say it seemed to indicate, it didn't, whatever, *indicate* it at all. It said it, which was the point of the whole article. And anyways, my landlord, in his message, he was trying to explain to me why the research was wrong-headed. Not in the piece, I mean *my* research. And the article was part of illuminating that. And he was just, he was very convincing."

She pushed her long hair back behind her ears. Her waist-length, chocolate hair was the single oracular element about her, the only whiff of supernatural insight or invincibility to the process. There was a primeval authority in such impractical hair. In the right light, I could get the impression that everyone *else*'s calendars were wrong.

I waited for her to pronounce on the enormity of my victory, to pounce on the importance of this great step forward. There would be some head-shaking amazement on her part about my strength, a search for words that were fit to describe my courage.

"One thing that we liked about your research was that it was getting you out of the house a lot," she said instead, calmly. "If that's suddenly cut out, I'm a little worried about you not having the same impetus to wake up, get out of the house, and have some place to travel to. Is there a way to deal with that?"

"Yeah," I said, beginning to explain that I could start adding workdays to my week, that in fact I could use the extra money. But as I spoke I tried to process her reaction. I couldn't believe how easily she'd shifted to this mundane concern about leaving the house. The night before, I'd imagined all the permutations of her possible responses — wide eyes, muted applause, ecstasy, pride over the patient's breakthrough — but this sort of indifference, shifting so instantaneously onto the next little utilitarian point hadn't come to mind as a possibility.

"Shouldn't we, like, take a second or something?"

"Sorry?"

"I mean, Jesus," I said, frustration creeping into my voice. "It's sort of big news, isn't it? Shouldn't we take a minute to assess what a big deal it is? I was doing this crazy thing, and it was taking up all of my time, and now I'm out the other end, aren't I, and we just passed over it so fucking quickly."

"Daniel, I'm sorry if I gave you the impression of indifference, or if I didn't give you the space you wanted to talk about your decision," she said, clearly floored by my anger. She softened her posture, glowing with gentleness and warmth. "Is there anything in particular you wanted to discuss about it?"

I sat forward in my seat, ran my hand up behind my ear and neck, pursed my lips, and then gulped air, sputtering, mortified.

"No."

My embarrassment laid me out in the same shade as Gary's politics, and I could see the doctor reverting to an instinctive, pre-Hippocratic need to help, a method of reaching out that predated her training, a charity that came not from a medic's oath to cure sicknesses and pathologies, but a person's desire to make another one feel safer, less foolish. Faced with her sudden monopoly on all the dignity in the room, she forfeited, and without making a show of her generosity.

"I heard a joke you might like, Daniel."

"What?" I felt cruel for my evinced suspicion, but Dr. Poitras is not a natural comedian. I can imagine her stepping on her own punchlines at parties, failing to carry a comic accent or simply losing the narrative thread of a joke. The likely failure of her joke makes the telling, now, all the more selfless; just as I've stumbled into this moment of prostrate idiocy she stands up to claim that she, too, is Spartacus, camouflaging my embarrassing moment against her own like those kids who shave their heads when a classmate gets chemo.

"A joke. It seems — well, did you hear about the anarchist obsessive-compulsive who thought that property was theft?"

"No," I bit.

"He was constantly checking to make sure he left the door unlocked."

On the bus home, I tried reading a campus newspaper, but the starts and stops and fogged windows made me nauseous and instead, I leaned my head against the window and closed my eyes. Without ever having fallen asleep on a plane or in a car, I somehow sank into sleep on this bus, waking up at Broadway and Commercial with an erection, feeling sick, dizzy, and disoriented. More than anything I wanted to take a cab home from the bus stop, to avoid the twelve-block walk, but I wasn't getting paid for another week.

The same week, it turned out, as Nicole's heart attack.

○

*Tom Nazir (news anchor): A clash erupted on Davie Street today between gay activists and multi-faith advocates of family values in a controversy surrounding a same-sex themed children's book that some parents want banned from Surrey schools. Reporter Nancy Kipling was in Vancouver's West End earlier today to witness the explosive scene. Nancy?*

*Nancy Kipling (reporter): Shelley and Slowey, two primary-coloured lesbian turtles sharing a single shell in Vancouver children's author Nicole Birnie's same-sex themed book, Turtledoves, have shell-shocked the Lower Mainland with a long-standing controversy in a way that Teenage Mutant Ninjas never could.*

*Roger Gerry (white everyman; citizen): We're here today to* voice our emphatic support for the idea that the parent's role in explaining sexual morality is sacred. No matter where we come from in the world originally, no matter our religious persuasion, we've come to Canada to raise our children freely, and we demand tolerance for faith-based morality and traditional values.

Nancy Kipling (objective observer): Pastor Roger Gerry spoke on behalf of the newly formed Multi-Faith Family Rights Coalition, an organization encompassing various Christian, Muslim, and Sikh groups who feel sex education belongs in the home, handled by parents.

Roger Gerry (parent, community member): I don't begrudge anyone the right to teach whichever lifestyle they want to their children. At the same time, government has no right to dictate the sexual morality of the citizenry.

Adnan Mufti (model minority; grateful immigrant): I am arrived to this beautiful country to raise my children in freedom, where government cannot take my children to be brainwashed. Our beliefs must be respected.

Nancy Kipling (storyteller): But defenders of the book, including its author, argue that it's Turtledoves that makes the case for tolerance and respect for diversity.

Nicole Birnie (bull dyke; professional protester): Turtledoves is at root a story about finding comfort; finding, defining, and redefining our notion of "home." Over the course of the story, Shelley and Slowey encounter many different friends, different animals, who each live in different kinds of homes, none of which suits the two turtles, but each of which suits their dwellers perfectly. The lesson to be drawn is exactly one of tolerance.

Nancy Kipling (witness to a decaying society): The two sides of this heated controversy engaged in an acrimonious debate all along Davie Street this afternoon, as the Family Rights Coalition *dogged a pro-*Turtledoves *march planned by the Purple Page, Vancouver's largest gay and lesbian bookstore. Surrey School officials are expecting to hand down a decision on the book early next month. Nancy Kipling, TV-West News, Vancouver.*

*Tom Nazir (man of the house): Thank you, Nancy.*

It was three or four hours later, after the broadcast, that Nicole began complaining of an overwhelming thirst. Soon, a shooting numbness colonized her left arm and Sara ran to the cabinet over the bathroom sink for aspirin, while with the thumb of her free hand dialing 9-1-1 on the cordless phone she'd retrieved from Robeson's dresser. Later, when things cleared up a bit, Sara worried that she had compounded Robeson's trauma by screaming at him to get down the hall, into his room, that his wailing and crying were making things worse. She begged him to run downstairs and unlock the door so that the paramedics could come in when they arrived. She cursed her choice of words when she saw his confusion, shouting "Ambulance drivers!" in explanation. "The people who'll take Mommy to the hospital."

The aspirin trick was the only thing Sara knew about treating the early moments of a heart attack. She sat on the floor cradling Nicole, who clutched her at her chest, exhaling pronouncedly through gritted teeth, tears falling out of the sides of her eyes and trickling back down in into her hair and ears.

"Hold on, baby," said Sara to Nicole and out loud, to herself. "The ambulance is coming, baby. You're going to be fine." She kissed her on the forehead and crown, repeatedly, with growing intensity that belied her quiet assurances. "You're going to be fine, baby. I know you will," she said, kissing her frantically, as an act of worship, as though she were a corpse.

At the Purple Page demonstration, I'd watched the reporter, Nancy Whatever, do two interviews that, had they been aired, might have delayed what I think was, admittedly, Nicole's inevitable attack.

*Sara MacDonald (mother): Absolutely, I'm proud of Nicole. I couldn't be prouder. I think that each of us is looking for someone who will build a world for us and for our children in which we feel safe and feel loved. She wrote a book – a beautiful, love-filled book – that makes my eight-year-old son feel at home. Her book makes him feel like the parents that he's known are in fact a part of the human experience, not some sick anomaly. She couldn't be a better parent: Instead of teaching our son to abide intimidation and hatred, she's making the world safer for him. She's trying. You're telling me that's not family values?*

*Gurmit Sihota (community leader): The so-called Multi-Faith Family Rights Coalition is nothing more than a very temporary alliance between prejudicial white racists and inorganic representatives of marginalized communities. I say inorganic because those of us in those communities remember all too well what Pastor Gerry's politics have meant for us over the years. He has never been a friend of our communities. Rather, we understand that it is in our interest to fight for the rights of all minority groups – including gay and lesbian communities, whose membership overlaps with ours, by the way – in times such as these when they're eroded. Let me say one other thing. These people claim to speak for the communities out in Surrey. But I was one of the main organizers of a multi-racial demonstration to defend our local hospital from closure in the face of budget cuts. Where were these "family values" community representatives then? Don't their families need hospital care? Further-*

more, *where were you? The media? Just who are the families of Surrey? How dare you frame them with such callous cruelty?*

I think the interviews were cut for time.

O

The Purple Page demo was the first time that I was certain Robeson was going to be straight. It wasn't only the way that he stared openly at Gurmit, watching the long, wide, black braid that hung down to her waist and shook as she pointed accusingly at the television cameras in the interview that never made it to air, or how he straightened nervously whenever she put her arms around him, gently calling him "*Bayta*," even kissing his cheek once as he reddened, instantly.

It was also a matter of logic, I thought, and felt guilty for thinking it. It was a matter of wondering — against the muted protestations of what was supposed to be my own belief that we're born with a sexuality that, while perhaps partly constructed, isn't one that we *choose* in any meaningful sense — why in God's name anyone who was making an educated decision would opt for the company of men over that of women? Why would anybody want the pissing contests and bravado and bullying of someone like Gerry, or the weakness and paralysis and privileged abstention of someone like me? Some people worry that gay couples might raise gay children, and besides thinking that that's a terrible thing to *worry* about, I'm convinced that there's nothing to it at all — which on final analysis is too bad, really, if you want to know the truth. I wish little girls *could* learn to grow up to be dykes just by watching their mothers not hitting each other. And raising boys? I sometimes wondered if the prospect of Good

Men — not just good, you know, like a handful of them, not just aberrations or guys on good days, but the eradication of Masculinity — could only ever happen if we stepped out of the picture of shaping young minds for a generation or two. There's not a question in my mind that Robeson will be a better person than I am, and I think it will mostly be a result of his being a worse man.

Certainly, he'd rather be in the company of women right now, instead of sitting on the couch in my basement suite, fighting off memories of *A Clockwork Orange* at the same time as he ruminates over his mother's surgery; his delicate confusion rushes me to the verge of tears. He's the next generation of little boys separated from their mothers by unknowing, by hospitals and paper masks.

I call out to him from my kitchen, where I'm pouring him some hot chocolate — well, pouring boiling water into a dry brown pile at the bottom of a mug that I've taken down from the cupboard for him.

"Robeson? You okay, buddy?" And then — fuck it — I drop the manliness, the junior machismo that intones men's conversations with little boys while we try to be father figures by emulating everything that's wrong with what fathers do. "You okay, Jelly Bean?"

"Uncle," he says, his voice raw from crying and affecting a disturbing maturity as he cocks his head to the side without changing the fixedness of his gaze on the wall. "You remember the peace-makers you were talking about?"

"You mean the pacemakers, sweetie?" I answer, bringing the hot chocolate into the room, setting it down on the coffee table and putting my arms around his shoulders, kissing the hair on top of his head.

"Yeah, pacemakers. Are you going to get one for your brain, Uncle Daniel?"

"I don't think so, love."

"Is it because they don't truly work?"

"No, I don't think that's why. I don't know, Robeson. I don't know if they work."

"Oh," he says, his voice shaking again, about to collapse again. "Because Mommy will be getting one. But that one is in her heart, not her brain. Will Mommy's peace-maker work?"

"Oh, honey, of course it will. Of course it will."

"But how do they know?"

"Oh, sweetie, they just know," I start to answer, until the phone rings and, hoping that it's Sara from the hospital with good news, I signal to Robeson that I'll be right back. I watch his eyes register the index finger that lets him know the precise number of seconds that I'm to be gone, note the shaking hope that he's invested in the promise, and run to my room to answer the phone.

"Sara?"

"Daniel? It's me," says Bo, in the same raw voice as the boy's, as though they were conspiring across two octaves.

"Bo? Hey man, I can't really talk right now. Robeson's still here, Sara's at the hospital, and the kid is in rough shape. But we should talk soon, I've got some good news about the research."

"Gerry's son killed himself."

"What?"

"The pastor. His son — it looks like it, anyway. The skinny kid. He's dead, and apparently it all seems really — the cops aren't giving any real details yet or whatever, but the subtext, the implication that I got, anyway, is that the kid was gay and that he killed himself. That's what it sounded like to me. I mean, the neighbours are telling reporters that they heard fighting over at the house before the family left for the demonstration, then they all heard the sirens and saw the fire trucks and the ambulances, and I guess the cameras showed up almost right away."

"Was he — was the son at the rally?"

"No."

"Jesus Christ."

"Yeah."

"Fuck."

We sat quietly for a second, me forgetting Robeson in the living room with his hot chocolate, Bo breathing rhythmically into the receiver. As sometimes happens in moments of tragedy — happens more than we'd like to admit, at least — distasteful, utilitarian concern reared its head and made itself heard.

"I guess," I ventured almost involuntarily, feeling tasteless even as I said it, "Gerry can't possibly keep up the campaign, can he?"

"I doubt it," Bo answered, quickly enough that I knew he'd considered it as well, alleviating some of my guilt.

We sat for another dozen seconds in reflection timed to Bo's breathy metronome.

"Daniel," he said, finally.

"What?"

"Is it — am I a shitty guy if I change the subject? There's just — there's one other thing, and I thought you might get a kick out of it."

"No, of course."

"I feel a little bit guilty, you know? Is it tacky to bring something else up?"

"Dude, just — don't worry."

"I won't keep you on the phone; I know you've got Robeson there. But you remember that night, in Kits, when you lost it on that comedian?"

"The homophobe?"

"Yeah."

"Yeah, I remember that."

"Saw him on TV tonight. The comic. He did the local — the talk show."

"What do you call it, the lady with the chest?"

"Yeah, that's the one," Bo laughed.

"*Urban Café*, it's called."

"*Urban Café*. Always with the 'Urban' in this fucking town."

"No shitting you, the other day, I saw a furniture shop called 'Urban City'."

"Urban City," he laughed, softly. "Fucking hell."

"Anyhow, *Urban Café*."

"The comic, he was on. Did a few minutes of stand-up, then the interview. He's writing a book."

"What do you mean — he wrote a book?"

"Writing one, yeah. Yeah. You remember when Al Sampson had that car crash, and he was in a coma and shit, and blah blah blah?"

"Yeah."

"That comic, he was the fucking guy who did Sampson's voice-over work while he was out. I guess — like these cartoons, they pay soundalike guys as an insurance against their voice actors. And this guy, apparently, he's an accomplished impressionist, and so he was hired to cover for Sampson, and when Sampson got better, he was out on his ass. Went through a whole depression, like, realized that he'd been living off another man's misery. Now he's writing a book about it, and so they were interviewing him."

"'Cause he's from Vancouver."

"I guess, yeah. Plus Sampson's from Edmonton."

"That's fucking — so the guy's just what? A parasite, then. First he's making money off the guy nearly dying, then he's making money off his getting better."

"I don't know that you've got to be that harsh about it, man. I thought of you when I heard it. It can be comforting. In a way, he turned things around for himself. Realized he had defined himself in terms, you know, of this guy's ill health. Now he's found a healthier place. He's defining himself in terms of another man's healing."

"Is that — did he say that?"

"Fuck no. He just said, 'Buy the book when it comes out.' I mean, he's still a fucking idiot. But it's nice." Bo paused. "Go look after Robeson."

"*Hanji. Sat sri akal ji, Birji.*"

"*Sat sri akal ji, Chotu.*"

"Love you."

"Love you, too."

I sat and stared at my feet for a minute until I heard Gary unlocking the door upstairs, about to discover, upon his homecoming, plants that I'd left dry for more than a week now. But don't let me define myself by the ill-health of plants.

I stood up and made my way to the living room, trailing my index finger along the edges of a reprint from the Winnipeg General Strike tacked up in the hallway, thinking of Gary and Bo, Sara and Nicole, Gurmit and Robeson. When I came into the living room, this last was looking up at me, expectantly, and I waved my hand at him to let him know it's okay, that wasn't the call, because I was scared that shaking my head would make him think, even just for a second, that his mother had died. The moment we saw Dad shaking his head, nothing but helplessness and surrender folded into his wet face, Marc and I had known that Mom was gone. The gesture had been an apology and an introduction to the world, revealed now as having always been stronger than our family. *The medicines couldn't help her*, my sweet and beaten father had said, shaking his head, disappearing every warm lie and comfort and looking to us for help, and I'd screamed, and I wouldn't do that to Robeson unless we had to.

"That was just a friend of mine, sweetie. No news from the hospital."

"Oh," he answered.

I sat down next to him, exhaled loudly and smiled in a way that didn't strain to be gentle, but still managed to be. I turned to face him, hold him, and he sunk his head into my shoulders and chest like the tide.

"Hon, I want you to promise me something."

"Okay."

"Honey, I want you to promise me that you won't worry at all about Mommy's medicine, or her operation, or her pacemaker, okay?"

"Okay."

"You ask me any question you want about people getting sick, and how they get better. I've read so much about it; I could almost be a doctor. Did you know that?"

"No."

"Well, it's true. I've read more stuff about medicines, and hospitals, and the machines that save people's lives than anybody I know. Did you know that, Jelly Bean?"

"Did you really read it?"

"I sure did, sweetie. And none of that reading means anything if I can't make it help, okay? Knowing things only means anything if it helps people, because a thought is just a thought if it stays inside. So you ask me whatever questions you want to know the answers to, and if I don't know them, then we'll find them together, okay?"

"Okay."

"And when your mommy gets home, sweetheart, she won't even believe how smart we are, how much we know about getting better."

**The End.**

# Acknowledgments

The two people to whom I'm most indebted for whatever works in this novel, as well as for its having seen the light of day, are my friends and editors, Anne Stone and George Fetherling. So: thank you, Anne and George.

I'm deeply grateful to the very good people at Insomniac Press for all of their work, including Mike O'Connor, sharp-eyed Gillian Rodgerson, and Dan Varrette. Many other friends and family members offered help, support, encouragement, quiet places to write, as well as critical eyes for earlier drafts. They are to be considered thanked after the following colon: Tejpal Singh Swatch, Derrick O'Keefe, Hiromi Goto, Dale McCartney, D'Arcy Saum, Tara Henley, Mark Leier, Annette DeFaveri, Russ Kennedy, David Chariandy, Paul Anthony, Peri Maric, Brian J. Wood, John K. Samson, B. Glen Rotchin, Shyla Seller, Morgan Brayton, Ian Rocksborough-Smith, Paul Bae, Wayde Compton, Graham Clark, Phil, Lynn, Laurie and Heather Birnie, Paul Arthur, Ellen Balka, Paul Hartmann, all the writers at the Legion (who inspire by osmosis), as well as Nicholas and Daniel Demers.

Like everything in my life, the experience of seeing this novel published is sweeter because I get to share it with my wife, Cara Ng, to whom and for whom I am eternally grateful.